“If you need

call. I don’t

Hank wished she did.... He’d never met anyone like Jolie.

She strode to the foyer and he followed at a respectable distance. She pressed down on the door handle and he moved forward then, so he could hold the door open for her. “Thank you. I can’t say it enough.”

His face was close to hers. He inhaled the light floral fragrance she wore.

She smiled at him, the right corner of her lips inching upward. “I like your kids.”

“And me?” The words seemed to blurt out of their own volition.

“You have enough on your plate. Keep things simple. Friends,” she stressed.

He didn’t want to be friends. He wanted to kiss her.

Dear Reader,

For a while now my editors have been asking me to write a book whose heroine is a teacher. Since I'm a romance writer by night/teacher by day, they figured I knew a bit about the subject.

But Jolie is no way based on me. First, she's a twin. Second, she's an elementary school teacher. Third, she falls in love with a man who has twins of his own. Nope, not even close to my life.

However, this book has become one of my favorites. Jolie and Hank are two people deserving a happily-ever-after. They've both been hurt by tragedy and they're both scared to put their emotions out there. They need to learn that when it comes to love they must open their hearts and take a risk. While life's not always easy, sometimes we get second chances that are even better than the first.

This book marks another milestone for me, as it's my twentieth novel for Harlequin Books. I'm glad it was Jolie and Hank's story. They're pretty special to me, and I hope you'll love them as much as I do.

Enjoy the romance,

Michele Dunaway

Twins for the Teacher

MICHELE DUNAWAY

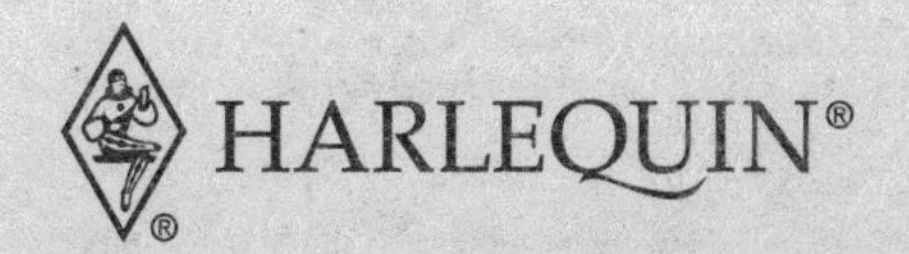

TORONTO • NEW YORK • LONDON
AMSTERDAM • PARIS • SYDNEY • HAMBURG
STOCKHOLM • ATHENS • TOKYO • MILAN • MADRID
PRAGUE • WARSAW • BUDAPEST • AUCKLAND

ISBN-13: 978-0-373-75255-3
ISBN-10: 0-373-75255-5

TWINS FOR THE TEACHER

This edition published by arrangement with Harlequin Books S.A.

www.eHarlequin.com

Printed in U.S.A.

ABOUT THE AUTHOR

In first grade Michele Dunaway knew she wanted to be a teacher when she grew up, and by second grade she knew she wanted to be an author. By third grade she was determined to be both, and before her high school class reunion, she'd succeeded. In addition to writing romance, Michele is a nationally recognized English and journalism educator who also advises both the yearbook and newspaper at her school. Born and raised in a west county suburb of St. Louis, Missouri, Michele has traveled extensively, with the cities and places she's visited often becoming settings for her stories. Described as a woman who does too much but doesn't ever want to stop, Michele gardens five acres in her spare time and shares her house with two tween daughters and six extremely lazy house cats that rule the roost.

Books by Michele Dunaway

HARLEQUIN AMERICAN ROMANCE

988—THE PLAYBOY'S PROTÉGÉE
1008—ABOUT LAST NIGHT...
1044—UNWRAPPING MR. WRIGHT
1056—EMERGENCY ENGAGEMENT
1100—LEGALLY TENDER
1116—CAPTURING THE COP
1127—THE MARRIAGE CAMPAIGN*
1144—THE WEDDING SECRET*
1158—NINE MONTHS' NOTICE*
1191—THE CHRISTMAS DATE
1207—THE MARRIAGE RECIPE

*American Beauties

First and foremost, to all my fans who have helped make this writing dream come true. Thank you. Next, to all my faraway friends, who are always in my heart: Karen Flynn, Jennifer Fly, Carrie Hilleary, Jenny Hassell and Julie Picraux. Even though we don't see each other often, we pick up as if it's yesterday. To Christy Janisse, Jo Anne Banker and Kay Hudson, who always make me feel like family. And for Joyce Adams Counts, whose friendship I would be remiss to forget, and to my mom, Louise Feager, for always being there.

And last but by no means least, for my new editor Laura Barth, who worked so hard to make this twenty-book milestone perfect. Thank you.

Chapter One

Enrolling your children in school should be easier than filing your federal taxes.

But it didn't feel that way to Hank Friesen as he sat outside the principal's office on a plastic chair two sizes too small for his six-foot frame and tried to register his ten-year-old twins in the fourth grade.

The secretary shot questions at him, rapid-fire. Yes, he knew it was April. Yes, their address was the Graham Nolter Resort and Conference Center and, yes, that *was* their permanent residence.

A lump formed in his throat as he continued to respond to the secretary's inquiry. No, there was no Mrs. Friesen. His wife died five years ago. No, his children had never before been enrolled in any other elementary school. Their maternal grandmother had homeschooled them these past five years.

Hank had also provided the secretary with immunization records and copies of Ethan's and Alli's birth certificates. He'd filled out emergency cards in triplicate. He was now working on a health history, the last form, he hoped, as his left hand was beginning to hurt. The secretary leaned over the old-fashioned laminate-and-metal counter to check on his progress before disappearing from view again.

"Are we going to see the classrooms, Dad?" Ethan, who'd arrived ten minutes before his twin sister, Alli, kicked his legs back and forth, making a loud thunk every time the soles of his tennis shoes connected with the metal rungs of the chair's under-the-seat book rack. He'd developed a distinctive rhythm, the staccato annoying and impossible to tune out. "So are we, Dad? Huh? Are we?"

"I don't know," Hank answered, wishing he'd brought the children's Nintendo DS handheld game systems along. That would have given them something to do while they waited. He'd assumed someone would at least give the kids a tour of their new school while he completed the necessary paperwork, but so far that hadn't happened.

He glanced at Alli. She'd bowed her head almost to her chest and sat with her hands folded in her lap. He had the urge to tickle her or something, anything to get her to crack a smile.

For a ten-year-old, Alli was far too serious. Unlike Ethan, she could sit perfectly still, prim and proper for hours on end. Where Ethan was rambunctious and boisterous, Alli was shy and demure. Ethan saw his dad's new resort-manager job as a grand adventure. Living in a hotel meant room service, endless indoor and outdoor pools and access to all sorts of fun activities like miniature golf and ice-cream-sundae bars.

Alli hadn't been as impressed. She'd assessed the hotel and their oversize suite with her quiet reserve before shrugging and saying, "It's okay."

Hank wanted to wake his daughter up, shake her out of the doldrums she'd mired herself in since they'd moved to Missouri a week earlier. His kids might have similar features—blond hair and blue eyes—but they were worlds apart.

Hank finished the form and stood. It felt great to stretch

his legs. Seeing he was ready, the secretary came over and thumbed through the stack of papers. "It looks like everything's in order," she said.

"So they can start Monday?" he asked. He'd used the resort's child-care services this week. He'd wanted to have the kids with him immediately on his relocation, but he still had to go to work.

"I don't see why not," she said. "Let me get you a school-supply list and..."

A woman walked into the office then, a teacher, Hank surmised, since the building had been locked for security purposes when they'd arrived and they'd had to be buzzed in.

She appeared to be in her thirties, a decade he'd left behind when he'd turned forty a few years ago. He was the class of 1982, Kickapoo High School, Springfield, Missouri. He'd been on the tennis team and student council with famous alumnus Brad Pitt.

The teacher stepped behind the counter and gave him a big smile, one she also directed toward his kids. "Hi," she said, tossing her long reddish-brown hair over her shoulders.

Hank automatically smiled back. Not only did she seem nice, but she was also very attractive. Something long dormant inside him flickered to life as he shook her hand. It was attraction, he realized with a start. If only he had time for such things, he might be tempted to flirt with her a little.

"Ah, Ms. Tomlinson, you'll probably be having one of these two. This is—" the secretary checked her paperwork "—Ethan and Alli Friesen. They're twins entering the fourth grade."

"Then one of you will be in my class," Ms. Tomlinson said with another radiant smile that Hank couldn't help but find fascinating. His fourth-grade teacher had been Mrs. Lemongrass. She'd been at least sixty. He had the urge to be a fourth grader again—but only if he could be in Ms. Tomlinson's class.

Ethan stopped kicking his feet and stood. "I'm the oldest."

Ms. Tomlinson's soft green eyes sparkled with amusement. "You must be Ethan. Nice to meet you. And this is your sister—"

"Alli," Hank filled in. His daughter had stood up, but social awkwardness had kept her from opening her mouth.

Ms. Tomlinson didn't seem to mind Alli's silence. "I'm glad you're here, Alli," she said warmly. "Welcome to Nolter Elementary. If you aren't in my class, you'll have Mrs. Hillhouse. We all call her Mrs. H."

Ms. Tomlinson reached out her hand, which was long and slender. As she waited for him to offer her his hand, she stared him in the eye, meaning she was just about as tall as he was. Few women were, and Hank was impressed by how well she carried herself. She was slim but toned, and looked as if she ran every day. "I'm Jolie Tomlinson," she said.

"Hank Friesen. I'm the new resort manager for the Nolter. We just relocated from Chicago."

He took her hand, appreciating the firm grip. He might be older, but he had the sudden impression she was wiser, that this was her area of expertise, like hotels were his. He felt better about his decision to enroll his children in a public school. He wanted them to be out in the real world, socializing with other children, as he had been at their age.

Now that he was back in southwestern Missouri, about sixty miles south of where he'd grown up and where his parents still lived, he wanted normalcy for his kids. At least as normal as you could get, living on-site at a top-notch destination hotel on the shores of Table Rock Lake.

"Well, welcome Hank, and Ethan and Alli. I'm looking

forward to working with you. My class is at art right now, so I'm on my plan time. Has anyone given you a tour?"

"We haven't seen anything but this office," Ethan inserted before his father could reply.

"That's because Mrs. Johnson, our counselor, is out of the building today at some very long and drab state meeting, as is our principal, Mrs. Jones. I hate meetings," Jolie said with a disgusted expression Hank assumed was for Ethan's benefit.

"Me, too," Ethan agreed, although he could have no idea what a meeting was like, having never been to one. Hank, however, had no less than three a day.

Jolie glanced at the clock on the wall. "I have ten minutes, so if we make this quick I can take you."

She handed the secretary a single sheet of paper. "Will you make me twenty-four copies of this before we get back?"

"Not a problem," the secretary said, and Hank wondered if she'd agreed so readily because she was glad everyone was leaving her alone.

"So you're from Chicago?" Jolie asked as she opened the office door and led them out into the hall. Nolter Elementary was a single-story building designed in the shape of an E.

"Dad's originally from Springfield," Ethan said. "But we've lived in Chicago all my life. I'm not sure if I'm going to like Missouri."

"I've lived in Missouri my whole life and like it fine," Jolie reassured the boy.

"I live in a hotel now," Ethan added.

"We had a house in Chicago, but we're currently living at the Nolter," Hank explained. "I want the kids to settle in before doing any house-hunting."

"I've been to Chicago twice," Jolie said, showing them

the main corridor, onto which the library and the art and music rooms opened. "It's a great city."

"Dad worked at the hotel right by American Girl Place," Alli offered. Her speaking startled Hank. He ruffled his daughter's blond hair, so like her mother's. Hank himself had a full head of dark hair.

Jolie showed them the cafeteria next. "Lunch is two dollars and you can set up an account that we automatically debit. Or kids can bring lunch from home. So, Alli, do you have any American Girl dolls?"

"I have Kristen, Felicity and one made to look like me," she said.

"I always liked Kit. That's the one I have," Jolie said, and Hank was impressed by her ability to make such an immediate connection with his shy daughter.

"I've read a book about Kit," Alli said.

"Good. We have many of the American Girl books in the library here. So—you like to read."

"I know *I* do. Goosebumps are the best!" Ethan shouted as Jolie opened a door. Hank noticed that Alli fell silent the moment her brother spoke and overshadowed her. Hank made a mental note to do something about that.

"This is my classroom," Jolie said, stepping to the side and letting them enter.

Hank hadn't been in an elementary school since he'd been a student, well over thirty years ago. Things had changed a lot since his time. A white marker board replaced the old green or black chalkboards he was familiar with. A SMART Board currently displayed a math equation. While the SMART Board screen was about the size of the old classroom pull-down movie screens Hank remembered, that's where the similarity ended. Using an LCD projector hooked up to the teacher's computer, the SMART Board became an interactive display. Each student desk had a handheld computer and a clicker, both of which could interact with the board.

"I wrote a grant for the handhelds," Ms. Tomlinson said. "Both fourth-grade classrooms have them. We even have wireless Internet on them. The clickers are for pop quizzes. They make the classroom like a game show. The children press in their responses to questions and the results come up on the SMART Board."

"Wow," Ethan breathed. "This is better than Grandmother's boring workbooks."

"They've been homeschooled until now," Hank explained.

"Missouri has quite a few students who are homeschooled. It's not uncommon, especially in this area. I'm sure they'll settle into public school with few difficulties," Jolie said.

Hank nodded as he watched his children explore their new environment. Alli was checking out the reading corner, which had carpet and beanbag chairs.

Jolie's next words caught everyone's attention. "Well, I need to go get my class from the art room, so that'll have to end our tour for today. Let me take you back to the office."

When they reached the office, she picked up the copies that were waiting on the counter and extended her hand again to shake Hank's. "It was nice to meet you." She pivoted slightly to address the children. "I'll see you two on Monday."

"Thank you for the tour," Alli said politely.

"Yeah, thanks," Ethan chimed in, belatedly remembering his manners.

Jolie smiled. "You are both very welcome. Thanks for the copies, Beth," she told the secretary before leaving the office.

"And here are copies of your paperwork, and our school

handbook," the secretary told Hank, handing him a folder. "Do you want to put anything in their lunch accounts?"

He hadn't thought that far ahead, but figured buying their lunches from the school cafeteria might help them fit in better. He also knew he wouldn't have time to pack brown-bag lunches, although he could probably have one of the hotel chefs whip something up.

"Sure," he said, taking out his checkbook. He wrote a check for one hundred dollars, putting fifty into each account. That should cover the rest of the school year.

Afterward, he ushered the twins out the school doors and back to the hotel. Deep down, he hoped this relocation worked out and he worried that it wouldn't. He'd received quite a promotion when he'd been named the Nolter's manager. The next step up the chain would be running a bigger hotel, like the one in New York or Paris, or even back in Chicago.

As it was, he had hundreds of employees under him, including various day managers, night managers, accountants, human resources personnel, cooks and groundskeepers. Everything at the hotel, in the minds of the brass at corporate headquarters, started and ended with him.

It was a job he'd been working more than twenty years for, ever since he'd graduated from college. The Premier Corporation had fifty hotels scattered all over the world. The company promoted management from within, rarely hiring outsiders over its existing employees.

Despite the opportunities to work abroad, Hank had always requested to be kept stateside because of his wife and children. He'd even turned down a promotion to Seattle after his wife, Amanda, had told him she really didn't want to leave Chicago and her parents.

Now, five years after her death from ovarian cancer, Hank finally felt strong enough to move forward with his life. He couldn't put his career aspirations on hold any longer. The Nolter job was the first step in making a fresh start for himself and the twins.

Hank slid his key card into the lock of their suite. He'd taken the four-bedroom suite in the east wing. The main portion of the hotel towered thirty-five stories and offered a fabulous view of Table Rock, one of Missouri's largest lakes.

The east and west wings of the hotel were fifteen stories tall, and their suite was on the top floor, with a view of both the lake and the golf course.

He glanced at his Rolex, a gift from the company when he'd received the promotion. Almost three. That meant Elsa, who sang in the hotel lounge at night and did child care during the day, would be available to babysit for a few hours. He'd promised the kids they could see a movie tonight, but that didn't start until seven-thirty. If Hank hurried, he could get his reports done today, instead of waiting until Monday.

"I'M GOING TO GET Ms. Tomlinson for a teacher," Ethan announced after their father left them yet again with Elsa.

Not that there was anything wrong with Elsa, Alli thought, ignoring her brother's bold comment. Elsa was pretty nice as babysitters went, not afraid to take them to the indoor water park or get her blond hair wet.

Alli had blond hair, too, and she'd always been a little afraid of the water because Grandmother said the chlorine could make her hair turn green. Now that Alli was ten, she'd learned there were "clarifying" shampoos that kept that from happening.

Alli pressed the controller on the video game she and her brother were playing. She'd wanted to go swimming, but Elsa said their dad was planning on taking them to the movie so they shouldn't get dirty.

How they would get dirty swimming in a pool was beyond Alli, and she figured that since Elsa was singing tonight she'd probably made it up. But her dad had told them he'd taken the whole day off. Once again, he'd lied.

Alli jutted her chin forward as Ethan's game character ran across and gathered up two of the gold coins spinning on the screen. "Hey, one of those should be mine," she protested.

"You should move faster then," Ethan retorted. Alli bit her lower lip. Ethan got everything. He always said it was because he was born first. Alli didn't know who'd decided to let her brother arrive before her, but she didn't like the results one bit.

"I think I'll play later," Alli said, getting up off the beanbag chair. She left Ethan's room, heading to her own. She had to admit that the hotel suite was okay.

She had a huge bedroom, her own bathroom, and she'd been allowed to bring most of her things from Chicago. Dad had even had the staff put a Playstation 3 in both her and Ethan's rooms, meaning they didn't have to share if they didn't want to. Aside from a computer in each of their bedrooms, there was also a family computer with Internet access out in the living area, which was bigger than the family room at their old house. Dad had said they might be able to have a small dog or cat after they were settled for a while. She'd never had a pet. Ethan, of course, wanted a dog, but Alli really wanted a kitten. She'd held one once at the pet store and fallen in love before she'd learned she had to put it back.

Alli flopped on her bed. "I don't care who I get," she told herself, thinking about school. She'd prefer Ms. Tomlinson, but Alli was simply happy to be going to school. She loved Grandmother, and Grandmother had taken them to all the museums in Chicago, but Alli was tired of only being around Ethan, not that she wanted to get rid of him or anything.

She liked the idea of being around other kids, even having friends who were girls her own age. And she'd be closer to her grandparents on her dad's side. Grandpa and Grandma Friesen were much more fun than her mom's parents.

In Chicago, every Sunday after church, Alli had dressed up in her finest and eaten lunch at some fancy restaurant. For once, she wanted to wear jeans on Sunday. Maybe this move would turn out to be a good thing, after all.

Chapter Two

"So, I heard you and I are each getting a new student," Carrie Hillhouse said Friday after school as she entered Jolie's classroom.

"You heard correctly." Jolie put aside the spelling tests she'd been grading so she could speak with the other fourth-grade teacher.

"Beth said they've been homeschooled by their grandmother their whole lives," Carrie said as she sat down. She glanced at Jolie's desk. "Ah, spelling. I gave my test yesterday. How are your kids doing?"

Jolie tapped the red pen on the desk once before setting it down. "Not too bad. The few who never study didn't this time, either. No surprise there. I think they have permanent spring fever. I'll reteach and retest. That will give Ethan a chance to catch up, anyway."

"Beth said you gave them a tour?" Carrie asked, toying with her wedding ring. She was young, three years out of college, and already married. She and Jolie had become close friends during the time they'd worked together. Jolie envied her. She'd been in love once, but it hadn't ended well.

"Yes, I met the father and the kids," Jolie offered. "They seem like a nice family." She shrugged, trying to stretch her shoulders. She'd been sitting grading papers for about twenty minutes. "Beth said he's a widower."

"Is he cute?" Carrie asked, grinning impishly.

"Never mind that," Jolie scolded gently. "We have bigger things to worry about."

"Yeah, I suppose you're right. With homeschooling they could be anywhere on the social and academic scale." Carrie voiced Jolie's unspoken fears. Some parents homeschooled their children and did a better job educating them than the local school district. Others used homeschooling as an excuse to be lazy, and their children were light-years behind other kids their age.

"They seem fine, but we'll see exactly how much they know once they start attacking the curriculum. I think this is a family that values education."

"Good." Carrie's relief was evident. Even after only a few years' teaching, she knew how hard it was to toss a new kid into the mix so close to the end of the school year. "So are you and Chad going out this weekend?"

Jolie shook her head. Her love life was starting to become a sore subject. "No. I think this thing with him has fizzled."

Chad had been Jolie's on-and-off boyfriend for the past year. She hadn't heard from him in about a week, probably because they were running out of things to say to each other.

"I'm sorry to hear that," Carrie said.

Jolie sighed. Chad owned a car-repair shop and they'd met when she'd needed new brakes. "Yeah, well, don't pity me. It's just a dent in my pretty nonexistent sex life. Not that he was that great, anyway. Heck, sex wasn't even great during my marriage. I'm in a lifelong dry spell."

"There's always the local bars," Carrie joked. "Or the sex-toy shop."

Jolie laughed. Trust Carrie to put things into perspective,

even if slightly skewed. "Perish the thought. I'm not that desperate yet!"

The women sat for a moment, each in her own thoughts. Then Carrie said, "I don't know how you do it. I mean that in a good way. I don't think I could be out there dating again."

Carrie had married her childhood sweetheart. Neither had ever gone out with anyone else after meeting in eighth grade.

"You just do it," Jolie said, picking up a stray blue pen and putting it in her desk drawer. "It's not what I planned for my life, but I've learned to take it as it comes. So get home to that guy and consider yourself lucky. I'll see you Monday."

"Sounds good. Don't work too hard." Carrie rose and left and Jolie finished grading her papers.

PAPERS WERE the bane of a teacher's existence, Jolie thought the next week while her class was at music. She pushed the stack aside, dreading the phone call she had to make.

"How are you doing?" Carrie asked, taking the chair next to Jolie's desk. Their plan time overlapped by ten minutes, so Carrie usually popped in after dropping her class off at phys ed.

"Getting ready to make a call," Jolie said.

Carrie winced. "Ethan?"

"Yep."

"I don't envy you. His sister is a dream. Be sure to tell their dad that. Maybe it'll soften the blow."

"Of what, telling him that Ethan..." Jolie stopped herself from saying aloud that Ethan was a monster. He really wasn't a bad kid, and she wasn't the type of teacher who gave up on anyone. But in four days, Ethan Friesen had so tried her patience she'd reached her tolerance limit.

Not that he was a horrible kid. Just misguided. He wasn't accustomed to the formal structure of school. He didn't see the reason for rules and pushed the envelope at every opportunity. Even Carrie, who taught history to both classes of fourth graders, was having difficulty keeping him under control. He liked to speak out, get up, wander around and he refused to comply with simple requests.

"It's probably just because he's used to being with his grandmother and not in a regular school environment. I'm going to request their Dad come in for a conference tomorrow afternoon if possible. Can you make it if it's right after school?"

Carrie thought for a second. "Yes. It would probably be best if we were both there."

"Then I'll let you know if I set it up." Jolie reached for the card she kept on each student, and, as if on cue, Carrie left the room to give her some privacy. Jolie dialed the number.

"Graham Nolter Resort and Conference Center," a bubbly voice answered. "How may I direct your call?"

"It's Jolie Tomlinson from Nolter Elementary. Will you please connect me with Hank Friesen?"

"Is this an emergency?" the girl asked.

"No," Jolie said, scanning the card for a cell-phone number or even an e-mail address.

"Please hold."

Thirty seconds passed before a deep voice answered the phone. "This is Hank Friesen."

Jolie had talked to a lot of parents, but for some reason she felt nervous with Hank on the other end of the line, and she was pretty sure it wasn't all because of Ethan. She forced herself to take a deep breath. "Hi, Mr. Friesen, this is Jolie Tomlinson. Is there any way you could meet me after school tomorrow for a parent-teacher conference? Ethan's off to a bit of a rough start and I'd like to be proactive and work with you on getting him settled in."

"You mean settled down, don't you?" She heard Hank sigh, as if he'd been expecting this to happen. "I know Ethan can be a handful. We've had babysitters who've refused to come back after spending one night caring for him. My mother-in-law had a handle on him, but she was, in my opinion, a little too indulgent."

"That may be," Jolie said, her tone sympathetic. No parent liked to hear that his child wasn't an angel, and it made her job easier that Hank seemed to be taking the news pretty well. Some parents became argumentative and immediately blamed the teacher for their child's problems.

Jolie relaxed her fingers. "I'm thinking that tomorrow afternoon we can come up with a plan that addresses Ethan's behavior. I'd like to set up some rewards and consequences for both school and home."

"And that will work?" He seemed hopeful, yet skeptical.

"In my experience I've found it to be a perfect starting point," she reassured him. "Having a behavior plan the child understands often ends many of the issues. I'm not saying it'll be an overnight transformation, but it will be a beginning."

"What time?" Hank asked.

"School dismisses at three. Could you do three-fifteen? That way Ethan and Alli are already at the latchkey program."

She heard a shuffle of papers. "Hmm… I have an appointment at three, but I'll have my assistant reschedule it." He paused. "I'll be there," he told her finally. "This is important."

More of her tension left. Even though she'd been contacting parents during the twelve years she'd been teaching, it never got easier. She only felt she'd developed more professionalism and understanding over the years. Parents wanted results and answers. Hopefully she could provide a little of both.

"Excellent. Thanks, Mr. Friesen. I'll see you tomorrow." With that she replaced the phone and sent an e-mail to Carrie saying the meeting was on.

HANK PRESSED the button, ending the call he'd taken via speakerphone after cutting short a meeting of the Nolter's day managers. They'd been about finished, anyway, so he doubted anyone was upset the meeting had ended early.

He exhaled, trying to ease the sense of foreboding taking root. As this week had unfolded, he'd hoped nothing was wrong. He'd convinced himself that the reason Ethan didn't have homework like his sister was because he was in a different class. Alli loved school already; Ethan claimed it was "okay." Alli raved about what she was learning; Ethan sat sullenly at the dinner table and said nothing, which was rare for a boy who normally overshadowed and outshouted his sister.

All the wishful thinking had been for naught. Hank had hoped his son's sullen behavior was a phase related to the adjustment of going to an actual school, instead of being taught by his grandmother. Hank had done research on Nolter Elementary, and it had won many educational awards.

Hank glanced at his personal organizer and then pressed the intercom button on his phone. His administrative assistant answered immediately. "I need to reschedule my three o'clock tomorrow. Tell Stan to bring me the full catering report at—" Hank flipped the pages of the planner "—eight forty-five on Monday. As for me, mark me as off-site as of two-thirty tomorrow afternoon. If it's an emergency, you can reach me on my pager."

"Will do," she said, disconnecting.

Hank picked up the five-by-seven framed portrait in front of him and leaned back in his chair. It was the last picture taken of the entire family, right after Ethan and Alli had turned four. They'd had a formal portrait done; the entire family had dressed in blue so that they coordinated. Everyone smiled broadly and appeared extremely happy, but if you looked closely, you could see the hollow circles around Amanda's eyes.

She'd been so brave, so full of gentle spirit until the very end, which had been mercifully quick. Hank's throat constricted slightly and he touched her face, as if trying to run a finger down her cheek. Instead, he obliterated her face entirely, reminding him she was but a memory of what should have been. They'd deserved it all. They hadn't had enough time. Would they even be in this situation with Ethan if Amanda had lived? He'd lost the love of his life; his children had lost their mother. Everyone, especially Amanda, had lost the future they'd deserved.

No one ever said life was fair. Hank had learned that lesson many times over. He forced away the melancholy and returned the frame to its place between recent pictures of Ethan and Alli. He had to focus on the future, not on the hopes and dreams they'd all lost.

He was doing the best he could to manage without her, and, damn it, his efforts had to be enough.

Chapter Three

Hank had never attended a parent-teacher conference before. As he strode across the parking lot, he received a few odd glances from mothers in cars waiting to pick up their children.

The few male teachers who taught at Nolter probably didn't dress in business suits. Maybe the mothers thought he was a book salesman or something.

Hank grimaced as he entered the building. He'd thought about changing first, but he'd run out of time as his meeting with the head accountant had run late. Time was one of those things Hank never seemed to have enough of, no matter how well he delegated.

Besides, he was comfortable in his attire. America had gone casual, and a suit still said class and power. That gave him a sense of security in this unfamiliar territory he was entering. He stepped into the office and announced to the secretary he had a meeting with Jolie Tomlinson.

The secretary had him sign in on a form. "She's expecting you. Just go down to her classroom. Do you remember the way?"

Hank nodded. He found Jolie Tomlinson's room, knocked on the metal door frame and entered.

"Hi." She rose to her feet and wiped her hands on her denim jumper before offering him her hand. "I'm glad you could make it."

"Like I said, this is important," he replied. He took a breath and tried to relax his shoulders.

She nodded. "Of course. I can tell you are a man who cares very deeply for his children."

Were there parents who simply didn't care and wouldn't show up? Hank wondered. The thought was appalling, but he remembered news reports he'd read while living in Chicago and realized that sadly, such parents did exist.

"So what seems to be Ethan's main problem?" Hank asked, cutting to the chase and steeling himself for the worst. She'd gestured to an adult-size chair placed in front of her desk. He sat. About four feet separated them.

"Ethan is having a few issues accepting authority. He has a very dominant personality. He can't shout out the answers to every question. He needs to share playground toys. When a teacher asks him to do something, he should do it immediately. Ethan has had to have a few time-outs for failing to meet class expectations."

Hank understood the concept of time-out, which was when a student was removed from the group. "So are these punishments during class?"

"We like to think of them as consequences and, no, they happen at recess. We operate on a check system. First check is a warning. Second check a student loses five minutes of recess, and the third check ten. Four checks is the whole recess and five checks means the child is sent to the office."

"How many check marks has Ethan had?"

"I keep track of them on this clipboard." Jolie passed a clipboard over and Hank saw today's sheet. At least, aside from Ethan, there were two other children on the list.

"Yesterday he had four check marks. I kept him inside during the entire twenty-minute afternoon recess. Instead of sitting quietly or reading, he kicked the underside of his desk the entire time. He's also not doing any homework. This morning I found a lot of the workbook pages I assigned wadded up in his backpack."

"I wondered about that. Alli seems to have at least a half hour of homework every night and Ethan always says he has none."

"Carrie Hillhouse and I do a lot of team teaching. She'd planned to attend this meeting, but she had an emergency. She teaches my class social studies, for example, and I teach hers science. We do a lot of the same lessons and we're planning to take both our classes on a field trip to the Shepherd of the Hills fish hatchery just below the Table Rock Dam the second week of May. We're studying pond and river habitats, and the hatchery is the largest trout-production facility in Missouri. I'd hate for Ethan to not be able to join us."

Hank knew many hotel guests visited the site, but he hadn't yet been there himself. He hadn't done any Branson shows either, and Branson had more theater seats than Broadway in New York City. "I think Ethan would like to see the fish," Hank said.

Jolie brushed a loose tendril of hair from her face. Her hair was a soft brown that looked almost auburn in the light of her desk lamp. And Hank wondered how silky it would feel. As he had the first time he'd seen her, he couldn't help noticing that Jolie Tomlinson was extremely attractive. He had the sudden urge to find out... He shook his head. She was his kids' teacher. What was he thinking?

"Yes, Ethan has told me he wants to go on the trip," Jolie responded. "And I think we can use the trip as extra incentive for him to improve his behavior. Your son is a very smart boy.

"He loves to read, so that's not a problem area. I tested him in math, and he's low. But not too low," she added quickly. "I think it's more that his grandmother didn't teach him a few concepts other kids his age learn, rather than any lack of ability on Ethan's part. Some after-school tutoring would bring him up to grade level by the end of the year. I'm confident he'll catch on quickly."

"Will that be available during latchkey?" Hank asked, suddenly overwhelmed by everything. They had yet to discuss the behavior plan.

He ran a hand through his hair, pushing it back off his face. Fatherhood didn't come with an instruction manual, and at the moment Hank really wished it did. Luckily it seemed that Jolie had the answer. She was the professional and he needed her help. "Just tell me what I need to do."

SHE WAS LOSING him. She'd seen the eyes of many a parent glaze over when discussing their children's problems.

She knew the symptoms. The parents, or parent in this case, were well-adjusted people. They held good jobs, made decent money. They loved their offspring and weren't abusive or neglectful. So how could they have children who had issues? They always figured she somehow knew all the answers.

Unfortunately neither of her college degrees came with magic wands. Still, she'd been taught some solutions and developed tenacity. You kept applying various strategies until one clicked. Something about Hank made her desire to help even stronger than usual. Maybe she was simply a sucker for a handsome face.

No, that wasn't it. She empathized with his plight. She wanted the best for him and his kids, the same thing she wanted for all her students and their parents. She reassured herself her motives were purely professional.

"Mr. Friesen," she began, careful of the words she used. "Ethan is a ten-year-old boy. He's not showing any signs of anything but being a normal boy who hasn't grown up attending regular school. I'm planning on working with him after school to teach him math. I also think this will help with some of the behavior issues, as he'll be getting extra face time with me. I suspect some of the motivation behind his behavior is that he wants my attention and is willing to do negative things to get it. If he can have my attention in a positive way, such as in a one-on-one tutoring session, that should reduce his outbursts."

"So that's math. How will the behavior plan work?" Hank asked.

"I have a copy of the plan I use with another student. I will be tweaking it slightly for Ethan."

Jolie handed him the sheet of paper. "Basically for every half day Ethan goes without a check mark, he earns one point. At the end of the week he should have ten points. You'll see the redemption chart at the bottom of the page. The first reward, which is five minutes extra recess time, is achievable after ten points. If he gets a check mark, he doesn't lose his previous points, but it will take him longer to earn the reward, since he won't earn any points when he gets a check."

"Do you think he can go a week?" Hank asked. His gray eyes held her gaze. He had nice eyes… She blinked and glanced away.

"I'm going to allow Ethan to earn the first reward after six points or three days. It's a teaser, but like a free month of cable or Internet, the reward is designed to hook you into using the program and staying with it."

Hank nodded. "What about home?"

He hadn't objected, which was a huge positive. "I would

suggest that you reinforce everything I do here. For homework completion he earns one point. For each day with no checks he earns a point. Then place a value on something he really wants and have him earn it."

Hank frowned as he contemplated the plan. "Should I discipline him if he gets check marks at school?"

"That's up to you. I'm already giving him consequences here in the classroom. But taking away his video-game system or not letting him watch television until his homework is done or until he behaves the next day would tell him that you want him to act properly no matter where he is. The key is, you must be consistent. You can't back down. If you do, your plan and mine will fail."

"Do you have kids?" he asked.

The question caught her off guard and she swallowed hard. "No."

He waited, then continued speaking when she didn't say anything more. "I guess we can try this. We're already in a period of flux, so maybe some set guidelines would help. I know this is an unsettled time for the kids. They were five when their mother died of ovarian cancer. And their grandmother has played a huge role in raising them since then. This is our first real attempt at being just the three of us on our own."

Jolie nodded her encouragement, appreciating that he was opening up to her. He was a man of strong character, the kind of man she'd always hoped to marry. She smiled. "I understand and please be assured I'm going to do everything I can to help you. Knowing your background helps."

Hank's pager beeped. "Sorry." He removed the pager from his belt and pressed a button, frowning as he read the number. "This isn't good. Will you excuse me a moment? It's work."

"Certainly," Jolie said. Hank stood and headed to the hallway. Through the open door, she watched him take out his cell phone, make a call and pace as he gave instructions to whoever was on the other end. She could hear snippets of his side of the conversation now and then, something to do with a corporate report and some revenue figures.

Jolie reached forward and looked over the behavior plan she'd handed Hank. In her conversations with Ethan he'd often complained that his dad worked all the time. She frowned. Hank had been interrupted in the middle of a scheduled conference. Surely the hotel could survive without him for an hour.

Hank was obviously struggling, like many single parents, to make things work for his family. They'd probably all been happy once, before his wife's illness. Hank was the provider; his wife was probably the stay-at-home nurturer. And then the grandmother had replaced her in that role. Now it was just Hank, all by himself, living in a hotel where the job was twenty-four/seven, trying to help his children settle into a new town and a new life. He relied on staff for roles that should be filled by family. The balance was upset. Hank needed help to keep his little family together.

He finished his call and came back into the room. "I'm sorry about that," he apologized. "I cleared my afternoon, but emergencies come up. It goes with the territory, I guess."

She smiled sympathetically. "Are you going to be able to pick up the children after our meeting? Ethan mentioned that you'd said they might get to do something touristy tonight. He's worried that because of our talk he might not get to go."

"I'll sit down with him tomorrow and discuss everything. Tonight we have tickets to the Dolly Parton Dixie Stampede.

I heard it was good. All finger food and a trick-horseback-riding show."

"I haven't seen it, but, yes, it's supposed to be fantastic. I'd dress in jeans, though."

Hank's smile split his face and Jolie felt a slight pang of longing. While many men in their midforties were sporting beer bellies and bald spots, Hank had aged like George Clooney. He was like a fine wine, only getting better with age.

His hair was rich and thick. His gray eyes crinkled at the corners, but those tiny laugh lines only added character to his handsome face. She'd definitely be interested if she'd met him in another place and another time.

It was an unspoken rule that you didn't date your students' parents. Not that Hank would be interested in her, anyway. The man had enough baggage and complications in his life. If he did date, he'd probably choose someone more glamorous and worldly. She had no idea what his wife had been like, but if she was half as pretty as her daughter, she'd been beautiful.

"I'll wear jeans," Hank responded to her earlier comment. "Ethan and Alli don't know it yet, but they're going to be special guests and participate in one of the events."

"That sounds wonderful. Ethan will really like that. Even more, I think he'll enjoy spending time with you," Jolie said. "I'll be telling him about the behavior plan on Monday. When you talk to him tomorrow, feel free to let him know it's coming. The more you show your support for what I do here at school, the better."

"I'm happy to help in any way," Hank said. He reached for the copy of the plan, folded it in thirds and tucked it into an inside jacket pocket. He stood again, and Jolie noticed the cut of his suit. It certainly hadn't come off the rack as her brothers' suits had, and she thought the three Tomlinson boys looked pretty good all decked out. Hank was divine.

"Thank you for coming in," Jolie said, rising to her feet. She didn't tower over him, which made a nice change from a lot of the other men she met. Growing up, she'd endured plenty of jokes about the weather up there, and, no, she didn't play basketball. "If there's anything I can do, don't hesitate to let me know."

She reached into a business-card holder and handed him a card. "This is the direct line into my classroom. If I can't answer, you'll get my voice mail."

"Great." He handed her one of his cards. "The best way to reach me is to page me. My e-mail address and pager number are at the bottom."

"Thank you. I'll e-mail you Monday afternoon and let you know how the day goes."

"That sounds great." Hank reached out and shook her hand, and this time Jolie noticed how firm but gentle his grip was. A delicious shiver ran up her arm from the contact. "I appreciate everything you're doing for Ethan."

And with that, he was out the door. It was Friday and there were five weeks of school left before summer vacation. She had plenty to do, but for the first time in a long time, she was too distracted to think about work.

Hank had unnerved her. He was the kind of man she'd dreamed about long ago when she'd believed in fairy tales. And he was way out of her league.

"SO HOW'S SCHOOL going? Ready for summer break?"

"Am I ever not?" Jolie answered her mother with a chuckle. Jolie lifted the bowl of potato salad and trekked the short distance to the oversize screened-in porch where all the food would be set out. It was Sunday, two days after her conference with Hank, and the entire Tomlinson clan had gathered to celebrate her sister Jennifer's twenty-eighth birthday.

Located about twenty minutes north of Branson, the hundred-acre farm where Jolie had grown up had been in the Tomlinson family for three generations. Her older brother, Bill, had recently bought ten acres adjoining her parents' land and built a house for his wife and kids.

Ten of Jolie's nieces and nephews were running around. Three were Bill's, two were Jennifer's, four were her brother Clay's and one was her twin brother Lance's. The only child not moving was Lance and his wife's newest addition, ten-month-old Natalie, who slept in the battery-operated baby swing, oblivious to the noise around her. There were eleven grandchildren in all, one short of a dozen.

Jolie's nieces and nephews ranged in age from Natalie to Chris, who was turning twelve next weekend. That meant another party to attend, this time at Bill's house.

Through the screen, Jolie took a second to watch the kids run through the yard. She was the only one without children and a husband. Her parents hadn't liked her ex-husband much. He was a teacher, and her father, a retired superintendent of a nearby school district, had told Jolie after her divorce that, had Reggie applied to his district, he would never have hired him. Jolie still saw Reggie on occasion because he taught science at Nolter High School and coached the football team. He'd remarried and his wife stayed at home with their two young kids.

"So how's Chad?" Jennifer asked, entering the screen porch carrying a green-bean casserole.

"Over," Jolie said. "Sent him an e-mail last night, got one back this morning. Mutual dissolution via the Internet. No blood. No tears. I spent last night with the latest Nora Roberts novel."

"Probably better in the long run. He didn't really seem

to fit in here. He was far too stodgy. But now who are you going to take to Alison's wedding?"

"I hadn't thought about it," Jolie said. Their cousin Alison was marrying some big-shot banker in early June. Word was that dinner was sixty dollars a plate and at least 250 people would attend. "I'll probably just RSVP for one."

"You can't go alone to these things. Aunt Melanie told Mom they were doing seating charts and everything," Jen chided. "It's at the Nolter in the grand ballroom, so you know it'll be a very formal event."

"I can bring Carrie," Jolie suggested.

Jen shook her head. "You took Carrie to cousin Brian's wedding. You cannot keep dragging your female friends to these things. The reception is going to be hoity-toity. You know how Mom's sister always tries to outdo her. For Mom's sake you've got to bring someone who's male and hopefully attractive. Don't you have anyone who can be a mercy date?"

Hank Friesen's image popped into Jolie's head. As if. "Everyone I know is married now," Jolie said with a shrug. Such was her life. Most guys she'd dated in the past few years had ended up being best buddies, not long-term love interests. Maybe that came from having a twin brother, or more likely from a serious lack of chemistry.

"Well, you have to find someone. You have a little over a month. That should be plenty of time."

"Okay, I'll RSVP for two," Jolie conceded.

"Good." Jennifer's gaze caught something in the yard and she immediately began shouting at her seven-year-old daughter, Suzy. "Hey! Knock that off! Put that down!"

Suzy had gotten out the garden hose and was spraying some of the younger children, soaking them through. But they were laughing and running into the spray, and looked as if they were having a great time. "I guess it's a good thing the day's warm. Clay, come get your kids and make sure mine behaves. Mom, we're going to need some beach towels," Jennifer called as she went back inside.

Clay hadn't yet appeared to retrieve his kids, and Suzy seemed in no hurry to put down the hose or stop spraying her cousins, so Jolie stepped outside onto the back lawn to keep an eye on them. Suzy sprayed her cousins again.

"Suzy, your mom told you to put that away," Jolie said.

"Do I have to?" Suzy asked, turning to face Jolie, the hose and all its streaming water moving in sync with her.

Jolie jumped back as water splattered her white T-shirt and khaki shorts. "Suzy!"

"Oops!" Suzy's face scrunched up as she realized what she'd done.

"It's fine. Don't cry. Just put the hose down," Jolie said patiently.

Suzy dropped the offending green rubber object as all the other wet cousins gathered around her. "You soaked Aunt Jolie. You're gonna get in trouble," they all seemed to chorus.

The situation didn't improve when Clay arrived and assessed the scene. He worked to hold in his laughter at finding his sister soaked. "Cute bra, sis." He turned off the water at the spigot.

"You can be such a jerk." His wife, Lynn, had appeared, and she tossed Jolie one of the towels she'd brought.

"Thanks," Jolie said, praying her face stopped flaming. She wore basic beige, for goodness' sake.

"You're welcome." Lynn looked at her husband of ten years. "Get inside and go find some of the spare clothes your mother keeps. The food's all ready."

"Yes, ma'am." Clay winked at Jolie as he escaped.

"Are you mad at me?" a small voice asked. Wrapped in a towel, Suzy approached her aunt.

"Oh, sweetie, it was an accident." Jolie squatted down to Suzy's level. "I'm sure your grandma has clothes for me, too. I can wear one of her T-shirts."

Suzy's face lost some of its wariness. "She has big T-shirts."

Jolie pulled Suzy toward her and gave her a hug. "She does. The biggest."

"Okay. Inside." Jennifer had returned to retrieve her daughter. "But first..." she prompted.

"I'm sorry," Suzy said automatically.

Jolie gave her niece one final hug. "And I forgive you."

"She's going to wear one of Grandma's T-shirts," Suzy told her mom as they moved off.

With the towel wrapped around her midsection, Jolie followed everyone as her siblings gathered up their kids and moved onto the screened porch. When her father had added the structure, he'd made it supersize, and weather permitting, every family gathering was held there. She made her way to her parents' bedroom where she snagged a gray Reed Springs School District shirt from the walk-in closet.

She paused for a moment after she put it on. She wondered if Ethan and Alli had ever squirted each other with a hose or attended huge family events. She'd been unable to get the twins out of her mind. As a twin herself, she couldn't help feeling a special connection to them. It must be a little lonely with just the two of them. She and Lance had shared a womb, but once they'd been born they'd been kid two and three respectively in what would turn out to be a total sibling set of five, only a year to eighteen months between each of them.

As a child, when Jolie had first discovered the truth about

how human babies were made—being on a farm she'd always understood the animal process—she'd found it a bit gross that her mom had popped out her kids in such quick succession. Now that Jolie was older, she appreciated having a large family, especially one so tightly knit and close in age. Family gatherings occurred frequently, and Lance and Jennifer were two of her best friends and her greatest support system.

Ethan and Alli had been around each other so much they probably hadn't come to appreciate the special bond they shared as siblings and as twins. As Jolie stepped back onto the screened porch, she saw at least four kids right around Ethan and Alli's age. Perhaps she could introduce her nieces and nephews to Ethan and Alli, give them someone to play with.

Jolie shook her head. She was tutoring Hank's children after school on her own time. That was already going above and beyond her teaching contract. Taking the Friesen twins under her wing by introducing them to some new friends was not necessary.

But what could it hurt? a little voice inside her head asked. *You could help them.*

Jolie frowned. She hated that little voice. It often pestered her to death until it got its way. So what if she identified with the twins, understood their love-hate relationship with each other? They'd learn through experience, just as she and Lance had.

Her conscience couldn't be silenced. *It's only until the end of the year. Then they go to fifth grade. You'll be just a face in the hall, a former teacher, one remembered fondly. Think of all those nights your dad was gone on school-district business. You understand.*

"Jolie, you better get in line or you won't get any green beans," Clay called.

"There's more in the oven," their mother admonished him, and as Jolie went to get her plate, she tried to ignore her conscience.

"DADDY! WATCH ME!"

Hank set down the report he was reading and watched his daughter slide down the curvy slide into the hotel pool. The Nolter had opened its outdoor pool this weekend, which was perfect, since the weekend was unusually warm.

He clapped for Alli, then checked on Ethan's location. Under the watchful eye of the lifeguard, his son was diving off the diving board. Hank turned his attention back to his report, but finding his concentration shot, set it aside. So far his children had adjusted to life in Branson. Both had made friends. Their grades were coming along and Ethan's behavior had improved. They seemed to like school, and Hank attributed that to one person, Jolie Tomlinson.

He knew she'd gone well beyond the call of duty. Ethan and Alli raved about Jolie every day. Hank actually found himself looking forward to hearing the stories his twins told. In each, he tried to learn more about their pretty teacher.

Hank reached for the iced tea on the table next to him and took a long drink. He'd dated a few times after Amanda's death, but no one had captured his attention quite like Jolie, a woman completely off-limits.

"Dad? You ever going to come in?" Alli's head appeared at the edge of the pool, her gaze expectant. She hopped out and walked to him.

Hank set the glass down. He'd learned long ago that there were some things, like cancer, that you couldn't control.

Making time for his children was something he did have a say in. Alli shouldn't have to ask. He rose to his feet and gave his daughter a sideways glance. She seemed to anticipate his words for she giggled and started for the pool as he yelled, "Last one in's a rotten egg."

Chapter Four

The call from Hank Friesen came two weeks later, at five-fifty on a Thursday night.

"Thank goodness you're still there," were his first words.

"Mr. Friesen?" Although she'd only spoken with him briefly a few times since their face-to-face meeting, she'd recognize that deep voice anywhere. Today it held a touch of desperation.

"Call me Hank," he insisted. "I've been trying to get through to the latchkey program, but they don't have a phone number."

"No, they use the phone in the office," Jolie explained.

"That's closed," he stated.

Well, technically the door was open, but everyone had gone home. Jolie had a report due in a week for the state agency that provided her technology grant, so she'd stayed late to work on that.

She really needed to get a life beyond her four classroom walls.

Hank didn't mince words. "Look, I'm stuck in traffic. It's horrible on the strip, so I got off onto the red route. Maybe I'm on the blue. Whatever color it is, it's not moving, either. I'm going to be late picking up Ethan and Alli, but I'm on my way. Will you let them know? Whatever the cost, I'll pay it."

Branson, entertainment mecca of the Midwest, was known for its horrible traffic. The city had spent millions building new roads and color-coding them. Still, anything could cause a snag.

"How about I just go get Ethan and Alli and I'll keep them here with me? I'll prop the side door open with a rug. You'll see my car by the door. It's a powder-blue Prius."

"Will they let you take them? I didn't put you on the contact sheet."

"I get Ethan daily for after-school tutoring. It should be fine for me to check out Alli, as well. Just get here in one piece. Take your time. No heroics."

"Okay, thanks." He disconnected and Jolie rose to her feet. She needed a break from sitting and typing, anyway. When she reached the cafeteria, where the latchkey program was held, Mrs. Monahan was signing out her daughter, leaving only the Friesen twins. Ethan was tapping his fingers on the table and Alli had two crayons and some paper out. Everything else had been cleaned up.

"Hey, Sam. I'm taking Ethan and Alli. Their dad's stuck in traffic."

Sam Jackson, a seventysomething retired schoolteacher, blinked. "I'm not sure that's in the policy."

Jolie ignored the curious glance of the teenage latchkey assistant and gave Sam her best smile. "It'll be fine. I just spoke with their dad. You could call him on his cell and confirm. He's at least twenty minutes away. I don't want you two to have to stay. You have his cell on the paperwork?"

"I want to go with Ms. Tomlinson," Ethan declared. "It's boring at the end of the day. I don't want to just sit here." He kicked the underside of the table for emphasis and Jolie shot him The Look. He quieted immediately. Since the implementation of his behavior plan, he'd been much better. Still, Ethan struggled. No one changed overnight.

"I guess it's okay," Sam finally conceded, probably having no real desire to stay past 6:00 p.m. with an edgy Ethan.

"Great!" Ethan whooped. He was already on his feet and grabbing his backpack from the hook. Alli moved a lot more slowly, gathering up the crayons first.

"Where do I sign?" Jolie asked.

Soon she ushered Alli and Ethan into her classroom. "Both of you put your backpacks on the hooks. The custodian hasn't been in here yet, but that doesn't mean we can make a mess. Is everyone's homework done?"

"I finished in latchkey," Ethan announced.

"I have social studies to do, but I need the Internet," Alli said. "I'll do that at the hotel."

Jolie noted that Alli used the word *hotel,* not home. "Games are okay if you put them back. The reading center is always good. Off-limits are my computers, the handhelds and the art supplies. Any questions? I'm going to be working on my report if you need me. Don't hesitate to interrupt. I'm not so busy I can't stop."

Both children stared at her and then scattered, Alli to the reading area and Ethan to the games. Jolie went back to her computer.

About five minutes later Alli's plaintive voice cut through the silence. "Stop it, Ethan."

Jolie swiveled in her chair so she could assess the situation. Bored with playing games alone, Ethan had cleaned up and moved over to the reading area. He was currently humming some unidentifiable tune, distracting his sister from the book she'd chosen.

"Ethan, I need your help," Jolie called. He came over to her desk and she pointed. "See all those papers? They're for tomorrow. I would appreciate it if you'd put one of those on everyone's desk. That way they'll have them first thing in the morning."

Jolie watched as Ethan did as she asked. Her brother Lance had often gotten bored easily and would torment her. Unfortunately, having Ethan pass out papers was only going to last a minute or two. And they had at least ten more minutes to kill before Hank arrived.

Maybe the truth is you wouldn't make a very good mother.

This time her inner voice reflected something her ex-husband had said long ago, right before he'd filed for divorce. Sure, she'd wanted more kids, but she hadn't been ready. Not so soon after the tragedy….

Jolie frowned, stood and pushed the painful memory aside. Ethan had distributed the last paper and was bringing the extras to her desk. The fact was, at this time in her life, she was no longer a mother. She was a teacher. Educators learned how to improvise. She clicked the mouse, closing her saved document. She'd finish it later. She turned on the SMART board. "Why don't you draw me a picture?" she suggested.

"What of?" Ethan asked as he handed her the papers.

"I don't know. What do you like to draw? Surprise me," Jolie suggested. She walked over to where Alli sat reading an American Girl story. "Is that a good book?"

"I've read it before," Alli said.

"So you like it?" Jolie pressed. Carrie had said that Alli was quiet. She'd made a couple of friends, but she was the shy one in the group.

"It's okay," Alli said. "It's a Girls of Many Lands book. Cecile's afraid of being put in the Bastille. She ends up banished, but she gets sent to school at St. Cyr, instead."

"That's how the book ends," Jolie said, seeing the correlation Alli was making. "Do you think you've been banished?"

Alli shrugged. "I've been sent to school. I liked the first few days. But I thought it would be a lot different."

Jolie's concern rose. "You don't like school?"

"I don't know," Alli said. Her lip quivered slightly and then she blurted, "Mrs. H is great. But some of the boys are teasing me. They say I'm freaky 'cause I never went to school before."

"Does Mrs. H know?" Jolie said, not surprised when she saw Alli shake her head. Carrie would have quashed that nonsense immediately. Teachers received in-service training every fall on harassment and bullying, including how to spot it and stop it. One of the things Nolter Elementary prided itself on was its character-building program and being a place where everyone felt welcome.

"I don't want to tell her," Alli said. "Grandma told me this would happen, but I didn't want to believe it. She didn't want us to go."

"Of course she didn't," Jolie said, sitting down on the carpet. "Your grandmother loves you very much. I'm sure she misses you."

"I miss her." Her face scrunched up and a tear escaped before Alli bit back the rest of the waterworks. "She and Dad fought a lot before we moved. She told him he was being pigheaded and stupid. I'm not sure how he can have a pig head, but I'm sure it's not good. I know what stupid means."

Jolie kept her tone compassionate. "Your dad thought this would be a great change for you and your brother. A way for the three of you to be your own family."

Alli folded her hands in her lap. "I know...and we're closer to Grandma and Grandpa Friesen now. They're fun.

We haven't seen them yet, though. Dad's been too busy. I liked his old job better. We saw him more."

The voice in Jolie's head told her not to get involved, but it was too late, she knew. She already was. "My dad was gone a lot, too," Jolie said, her heart going out to the little girl.

"Really?" Alli's blue eyes widened.

Jolie nodded. "Yep. My dad was a superintendent. That means he ran the whole school district."

"So he was your boss," Alli said.

"No, he worked at a different school district and I wasn't a teacher yet. But he had to be at school-board meetings and community dinners. He also attended basketball games and school plays. He wasn't around much."

Alli stared at her hands. "Marissa says her dad works from home and she sees him all the time."

"That's because Marissa's dad is a real-estate agent and his main office is in his basement," Jolie said. "Lots of dads are gone. You know Joey in your class? His dad is in the army and he won't be back until August. He's in Iraq."

Alli appeared to think about that, her chin coming up so she could study Jolie's face.

"You still don't have to like it, though," Jolie said quickly.

Alli's brow creased as she absorbed this piece of information. "No?"

"No," Jolie confirmed. "You just have to know that your father loves you very much. That's the most important thing. He does love you or he wouldn't have called me, frantic, when he knew he was going to be late. Being a dad is hard work, especially in your case. He's doing double duty."

"I don't remember my mom much anymore," Alli confided. "I have pictures of her, though. She was blond, like me and Ethan."

"I'm sure your mom loved you very much, too. She's in heaven and probably very happy that your dad brought you here."

"My grandma said she wouldn't be." Alli's tone was matter-of-fact.

"Grandmas don't always know everything," Jolie said, not impressed that Alli's grandmother had burdened a ten-year-old with such a message. "Your mom would want your dad to be happy. He likes his new job, doesn't he?"

She gave a quick nod. "I think so. He said it's what he's always wanted."

"Well, doing a job you love is important. I love my job, too. And see, I'm here late."

"You don't have kids," Alli pointed out.

"No, I don't," Jolie said, the familiar pang of sadness washing over her. She brushed the feeling aside and concentrated. "But even if I did have kids, sometimes I would have to work late. Like Mrs. Monahan."

"She picks up Kelly right before latchkey closes every day. At least my dad's early sometimes. He tries to be there by five-fifteen," Alli said, giving her dad some credit.

"See?" Jolie said. "In Kelly's family, she lives only with her mom. Her mom has to work. You live only with your dad."

"I don't get why people have to work. No one seems to like it," Alli said.

Jolie sighed. Her siblings complained that their children thought money grew on trees. "People work to pay their bills. Things like houses, cars, clothes and food aren't free."

"Dad uses a charge card."

"You still have to pay that. Just all at once," Jolie said.

"Oh." Alli considered that.

"Dad!" Ethan shouted. "See what I made?"

Jolie swiveled her head to see Hank Friesen standing in

the doorway, as usual impeccable in his dark blue suit. She panned her gaze from him to the SMART board, where Ethan had drawn a picture of a boy playing baseball. He had some raw talent for cartooning.

"I hope they weren't too much trouble," Hank said, his gaze assessing Jolie and making her self-conscious.

Alli clambered to her feet and rushed over to her dad. Jolie stood.

"We've been good," Ethan announced. "I passed out papers to every desk and then got to draw on the SMART board."

"I guess that's a good perk," Hank said, hugging his daughter before catching Jolie's attention. He winked at Jolie and something inside her stomach danced. She placed a hand over the area to stop the sensation. "So what did *you* do?" he asked Alli.

"I read a book," she said.

"I hope it was good." Hank smiled.

"I've read it before. It's okay," Alli said.

"Go get your stuff off the hooks," Jolie instructed, deciding to take charge. Hank's presence had unsettled her. He was too attractive for his own good, like a sweet displayed in a bakery window. Too bad she couldn't indulge.

Ethan and Alli rushed to do as she'd asked.

"Thank you," Hank said, stepping toward Jolie. "Turns out there was a three-car accident, which is why traffic was all tied up."

"It'll take forever for the mess to clear, then," Jolie replied, trying to calm her heartbeat. Hank was off-limits.

"I know. I figured I'd take the kids out to dinner before trying to get back. It's snarled in both directions. All we'll do is sit in a bumper-to-bumper jam again."

"Eating's a good idea. The last snack they had was at three-thirty."

"It was only a cookie and some apple juice," Ethan inserted as he bounced up with his backpack in tow. "We didn't get seconds because Sam didn't have enough for everyone. I'm hungry. Let's go to McDonald's."

"I'm sick of McDonald's. You always have to eat there. I want to go somewhere I like for a change," Alli protested. "Dad, can I pick? Ethan always picks."

"I don't like where you like," Ethan argued. "I want some McNuggets."

"Well, I don't. Da-ad," Alli whined.

"I was thinking we'd go someplace where you sit down with menus," Hank tried.

"That's just like at the hotel," Ethan said. "I'm tired of sitting in the restaurant. I want drive-thru."

"I don't," Hank said.

"I don't want to eat where your food comes out through a window unless it's Arby's," Alli said. "I want roast beef."

"You two are worse than my brother Lance and I ever were," Jolie interrupted. Her teacher-voice chastisement had both children staring at her. "Your dad just drove through traffic and there was an accident. Everyone's hungry and you can't get home for a while. Sitting down someplace might be good. My family and I always sat at a table. We did not eat in the backseat of a car."

"I'm tired of fancy," Ethan said, and Hank rolled his eyes heavenward.

"I'm tired of this debate," Hank said. He glanced at Jolie. "Is there a place you'd suggest? We have at least an hour to kill."

"Can you stand Chuck E. Cheese's?" she asked.

That caught the kids' attention. Chuck E. Cheese's was a child mecca, with games to play and prizes to win.

"We haven't been there forever, Dad," Ethan said.

"You like the skeeball game," Alli chimed in. Now that she and her brother were on the same page, they worked together to convince their dad.

"I guess Chuck E. Cheese's is fine," Hank said, although it was obvious he wasn't excited about the choice.

Jolie smiled. "Probably not what you'd hoped for, but a good compromise."

"It's noisy. I won't be able to hear anything if anyone calls. I guess I could text."

"That's the spirit." Jolie moved behind her desk and shut down her computer. She might as well leave. By the time she got home and got something to eat, it'd be late.

She heard some whispering as the kids stopped and talked to their dad just inside the doorway. She glanced over, expectant. "What's wrong?"

"Ethan and Alli would like you to join us," Hank told her.

"I'm not sure that's a good idea," Jolie said. Dinner with Hank seemed far too intimate and might be misinterpreted if anyone saw them.

"Please?" Ethan and Alli chimed at once.

"You could show us where it is, if nothing else. I'm not that familiar yet with this part of town," Hank said.

Alli tugged on her dad's suit jacket. "Don't they have a salad bar, Dad? Just in case you don't like pizza," Alli told Jolie, her smile hopeful.

"Please join us," Ethan said, trying manners as another tactic to cajole her.

At that moment Jolie's stomach rumbled. Eating dinner with a parent and his children pushed the boundaries, but she was hungry. She also wanted to talk to Hank about what Alli had said earlier. Besides, this wasn't a date or anything—although part of her wished it was. Hopefully spending time with Hank wouldn't be too torturous. She liked him and life wasn't playing fair. She had to keep the relationship professional.

"Only if I pay for my own dinner," she said.

"Yay!" the kids chorused as they raced out of the room and down the hall.

Hank hovered for a moment. "You're okay with this? You are saving me from sitting there alone, so trust me, I don't mind."

She arched an eyebrow in query. Even to this day, all her grown brothers still had to get tokens of their own. "You don't play the games?"

"It's easier to let Ethan and Alli run and enjoy themselves without me. Usually when we do stuff like this, I bring a book or do work."

"In that case, I'd actually like to talk with you. We can hold a follow-up conference in the booth. Ethan's been much better."

"That's good," Hank said. "I hear a *but* coming, though."

"It's not as bad as you think and we'll talk at the restaurant." She locked her classroom and they walked down the hall. Ethan and Alli were already outside in the big black Lexus sedan parked next to her tiny Prius.

She moved the rug out of the school doorway, letting the outside door close and lock. "I'll follow you," Hank said.

They reached their destination several minutes later. After entering and having their hands stamped with invisible ink, the group proceeded to the counter, where they ordered food and tokens for games. Although Jolie protested, Hank put the entire bill, including her unlimited-salad-bar order, on his credit card.

"You shouldn't have done that. I said I would pay for myself," she said, pulling her wallet out of her purse once they were sitting at a table.

"Put your money away. I can afford whatever it was.

What? Six dollars, tops? Consider it a teacher-appreciation gift." He waved off her money and took the receipt. Alli and Ethan each had sixty tokens and had taken off without even filling their soda cups.

Hank had left his suit coat in the car, and he'd ditched his tie. He'd unbuttoned his top two buttons and rolled up the cuffs on his sleeves. He'd lost that executive look, but none of the raw male appeal.

She shouldn't be thinking of him that way. Already she was close enough to smell his cologne.

She sat catty-corner to him. Otherwise, their long legs would be tangled together under the table, which was neither wise, nor appropriate. She'd already glanced around several times, worried that someone might recognize her and misconstrue the situation.

"So what did you want to talk about?" Hank asked.

Jolie took a deep breath and dove in. "First, as I said, Ethan's doing much better."

Hank appeared pleased. "Your plan has been a lifesaver. He's improved a lot at home, too. He's even tidied up his room each day rather than leave it a mess for the housekeeping staff."

"You have a service?"

Hank grinned. "One of the perks of living in the hotel. Although, I make sure all my private stuff is put away. They are employees, after all."

Maybe some really did live differently, Jolie thought. "What about bedtime routine? He doesn't seem as tired this past week."

"I've been able to be home and keep things consistent. Nine o'clock and lights-out."

"That's good. That's the time my brother puts his kids to sleep. Do you read to Ethan or anything?"

"No, but I do tuck him in and turn out the light. On even nights I go into Alli's room first and on odd I go into Ethan's. That's something Amanda started and I've tried to continue it." He saw Jolie's expression and elaborated, "Amanda was my wife."

"I assumed, but thanks for clarifying. All these things sound really great. What I wanted to tell you tonight is that Alli and I talked. I'm concerned that she's homesick for Chicago. She said she's missing her grandmother."

Hank's shoulders tightened and his cheeks had hollowed slightly. "I was afraid of that."

"She said she heard her grandmother tell you that moving here was a bad idea."

"Those weren't her exact words," Hank said ruefully. "She thought it was stupid for me to move out of Chicago. But I couldn't stay there anymore. The memories. The job. It was past time."

"You needed a fresh start," Jolie agreed.

"I don't know if you've ever lost someone, but it's rough. I'm hoping things get better as time goes on. While I think this move was for the better, I knew it wouldn't be easy. It's probably hardest on Alli because of her shyness. As you've seen, Ethan tends to overshadow her. I've been trying to get him to lighten up a little. How can they be twins but be nothing alike?"

"It's very common, actually. My twin brother and I are exact opposites in a lot of areas. He's athletic and played all the sports, while I'm the theater geek. He's good at all things English, whereas I'm better at math. He's a great cook and I'm terrible."

Hank settled against the booth, relaxing slightly. "I didn't know you were a twin."

"That's because I'm my own person and so is he. We

don't advertise it much. My mother had two more kids after she had Lance and me, so it's not like we got special attention. The only good thing, since I was the first girl, was I didn't have to wear hand-me-downs like Lance. I did have to share my room, though, once Jennifer come along. And a lot of girls befriended me just to get to my brothers."

Hank nodded. "I wonder if the same thing will happen to Alli. It's hard to imagine any girls being interested in Ethan just yet. Maybe in a few years. I didn't know much about twins or what to expect before Ethan and Alli came along. In my family there's only my sister and me. Jessie's five years younger and lives with her husband in upstate New York."

"Families are strange but wonderful things," Jolie remarked as an employee brought the large pizza Hank had ordered. As if sensing food, Alli and Ethan arrived within seconds and soon everyone had filled their drink cups. The twins each ate one slice of pizza and then rushed off to use more of their tokens. They covered much of the table with the tickets they'd won, their respective piles becoming more and more indistinguishable as the evening wore on. They also came back and ate a little more. While they were playing, Jolie told Hank more about her family, and he shared a bit more about his upbringing.

"Thanks for staying with the kids earlier and keeping me company," Hank said. He glanced at his watch. "We've been here about an hour and half. I probably should start getting them ready to go."

"Good idea." She pushed her salad plate away. "By the way, when Ethan and Alli return to the table, you might want to help them sort out their tickets. My brother always seemed to get more than I did. Maybe he won more things, but…"

Hank fingered three connected tickets. "Good idea. I'm

also going to go with them to the counter. The last thing we probably need are more fake-eyeball-gag toys. That's what Ethan got last time we went somewhere like this."

"Sounds like something Lance would have picked," Jolie said with a smile. "He'd leave fake plastic snakes around the house. We grew up on a farm, so there were plenty of real snakes to worry about, and he constantly freaked my mother out with his antics. At family gatherings she blames him for her gray hair."

"I wish I had someone to blame for mine," Hank said. He touched his hair, but Jolie didn't see any gray.

"If you don't mind my asking, how old are you?" Jolie asked.

"I'm forty-four. I was actually one of the younger graduates in my class," Hank replied. "Now I'm one of the youngest managers at the Premier Hotels Group. I've been with them since I graduated from college."

"Wow."

From his satisfied expression she could tell he was pleased with his accomplishment. "I've worked my way up."

"So you always wanted to be a hotel manager?"

"I'd rather do that than run the company," Hank said. "I like being in one place. The people who oversee everything travel at least seventy percent of the time. With this job I'll travel to the company headquarters in Chicago around annual-report time and for a few other occasions, but really not that much. We use video conferencing, instead."

"That does sound better for raising a family," Jolie said.

"Let me know if you're ever planning on going somewhere. I can get you deep discounts for some pretty posh places."

"I want to travel somewhere this summer but haven't decided. Thanks for the offer, but I doubt I'd be able to afford your chain even with the discount. I'm thinking about making the plunge next January and buying a house. I've been saving for years, but still need more for a down payment."

Hank frowned. "Don't they have first-time buyers programs in Missouri?"

"I lost that eligibility and half my assets in my divorce," Jolie said flatly.

"I'm sorry." Hank looked rueful. "I shouldn't have pried."

She shook her head. "No, it's okay. It was for the best, and it's ancient history, anyhow. I signed the divorce papers eight years ago."

At that moment Ethan and Alli came up and within ten minutes, they'd traded their tickets for merchandise. On the way out, they all had their hand stamps checked under the black light and soon they were out in the parking lot where Hank's big black sedan waited by her little hybrid.

Hank started his car with a remote and loaded the kids into the backseat before he turned to her. They stood between the cars, with Jolie next to her driver's side door. "Thanks for everything," he said again. "I don't have anyone here to help me in a pinch and I can't tell you how much I appreciate this." His voice caught slightly.

"It's nothing," Jolie said, wishing it was more. This had been one of the best non-dates she'd ever had. Tonight had been fun and Hank was great company.

He tilted his head. "It's not nothing. It's above and beyond your duties as a teacher and I truly do appreciate it. I'll try to find someone else next time, though, and not put you out again."

Something had her wanting to put his mind at ease. "It's no problem. If you need help, call me. I like your kids. I really don't mind. All of you could use a break." The last words slipped out before she could stop them.

"Thanks," Hank said. He stood there a bit awkwardly.

"It's not a problem," Jolie repeated. Her decision made almost subconsciously, she dug in her purse and pulled out the small notebook and pen she kept inside. She scrawled out a phone number. "That's my cell, which doubles as my home phone. If you have another crisis, call. I'm serious. I babysit my nieces and nephews all the time. You need someone to help you out, so it might as well be me." She couldn't date him, but she could do this, right?

"Thanks," Hank said, pocketing the number. "This means a lot."

She focused on acting casual. "Have a good night."

With that, Jolie got into her car and fired up the engine. She waved to the kids, pulled out of the parking lot and turned toward home. On the drive the second-guessing began. She'd given him her phone number. She doubted he'd call, but wanted him to do just that.

Everyone claimed she liked to torture herself by setting herself up in situations like this. She and Hank couldn't get involved. So she'd simply add him to her friends list, she decided. Her mother always helped people in need, and Jolie had been raised to do the same. There, that was a solution, she convinced herself.

Hank was a man who could desperately use some friends. While she wouldn't bake him a casserole, which was her mother's standard, she could help him out with his kids. Children were precious, and the twins needed her as much as Hank did.

Chapter Five

"I've received a summons to the principal's office after school," Jolie confided to Carrie during lunch the next day. They'd opted to eat in Carrie's classroom, instead of the staff lounge so that they could have total privacy. "She stopped by this morning to make the request in person."

Carrie frowned and began unpacking her lunch. "That's never good. She hates to come out of her office unless necessary. Did she mention what the meeting was for?"

"No, but I have a feeling it's about Hank Friesen." Jolie dumped out her paper sack and gazed down at the unappealing food she'd brought.

"Why would it be about him?" Carrie asked. She'd made a chicken-salad sandwich, and the aroma of pecans, mayonnaise and red grapes reached Jolie's nose.

Jolie pushed aside her own meal, a boring peanut-butter-and-jelly sandwich on slightly stale bread accompanied by a box of past-their-prime raisins. She'd planned on going grocery shopping last night, but by the time she left Chuck E. Cheese's, she hadn't felt like it.

"I went out to dinner with Hank and his kids," Jolie said, opting to forgo her lunch in favor of the packaged cookies she'd bought from the faculty-lounge vending machine.

"Well, don't keep me waiting—fill me in on what happened," Carrie said, gesturing with a carrot stick.

"Hank was running late. He called and asked me if I could let the latchkey people know. I offered to keep the twins with me in my classroom until he arrived. I was working, anyway, so it was no trouble."

Carrie nodded and held out her sandwich. "Do you want some of this?"

"I'm good," Jolie said, biting into another cookie as her stomach growled. She'd skipped breakfast and the pizza she'd eaten for dinner the night before was a distant memory, at least to her stomach. The memory of her time with Hank was as fresh as if it had occurred minutes ago.

Carrie kept eating. "So I don't get it. Principal Jones wants to see you about that?"

Jolie shook her head. "No. Probably what happened after. The kids invited me to dinner and I accepted. We all went to Chuck E. Cheese's. I guess someone saw us and called her. Sometimes this town can be way too small."

"Sure is," Carrie said. She put her sandwich down. "I really can't finish this. I made chicken for dinner a couple of days ago and have been eating leftovers ever since. Are you sure you don't want the rest? I'm only going to throw it away."

"If you're pitching it, sure," Jolie said, succumbing to her hunger.

Carrie passed her the sandwich. "So what will you do?"

Jolie took a bite. It was as delicious as it smelled and she hadn't had homemade chicken salad for ages. "I don't know. I guess the best recourse is to hear her out. I didn't do anything wrong. It wasn't a date. I'm not playing favorites."

"You have been tutoring Ethan," Carrie pointed out, playing devil's advocate.

"Yeah, but with the federal government breathing down the state's neck because of the No Child Left Behind Act, everyone's worried about test scores. I'm certainly not going to let those kids slip through the cracks. Besides, denying them help would be much more unprofessional than my going to dinner with their dad."

Carrie shrugged her agreement and ate more carrot sticks. Jolie made a mental note to buy some fresh fruit and vegetables. Of course, most of her purchase would probably go bad. She wasn't really a big eater and the pre-filled bags often contained enough for a small army.

"Well, good luck. If you need to call me at home tonight and vent, feel free," Carrie offered.

Jolie hoped it wouldn't come to that. "Thanks, but it should be okay. I didn't do anything wrong. It's not like it was a real date. Just a parent-teacher conference off campus."

"Hank Friesen is a pretty attractive guy, though," Carrie remarked.

Okay, that was an understatement. He'd been in her dreams last night. She hadn't wanted to wake up.

"I'll admit he is and I'm certainly not debating that. But I'm not interested, and even if I was, he's the parent of one of my students. I do have standards and can draw the line."

Besides, it wasn't as if he was interested in her, anyway, Jolie told herself. He had a relocation to deal with and a new job. Dating most likely wasn't high on his priority list. He appeared to be a man extremely devoted to his children, and Jolie knew firsthand how much attention children needed. Her own child… She bit her lip, trying to distract herself from the painful memory.

She usually tried to avoid thinking about Ruthie, but today she failed. Her little girl had been so full of life, with the bluest of eyes. Jolie had had an easy pregnancy. She and her husband had been so happy; even the delivery had been smooth. There had been Ruthie—ten fingers, ten toes and ten on her Apgar.

Everything had been great for the first month, apart from the lack of sleep and the round-the-clock schedule Jolie's body was on. Sure she'd forsaken her husband after the birth, but he'd understood, or so she'd thought. A baby was a precious gift. It didn't matter that she'd been so tired that night.

She'd had the monitor going, right by her ear on the nightstand. She should have known something was wrong when Ruthie didn't cry, but instead, Jolie had slept on, the silent monitor concealing tragedy.

The next morning her sweet Ruthie was gone, the official cause of death listed as SIDS—sudden infant death syndrome, or crib death. She'd never thought something like that would happen to her. Her husband had blamed her, but he needn't have bothered. Jolie blamed herself enough for both of them. No matter that SIDS was unpredictable and struck at random. She should have been more vigilant. She'd carried that guilt with her every day since Ruthie's death.

She took a steadying breath and turned to face Carrie. "I've been through much worse than whatever this meeting can bring," Jolie told her. "I'm sure it will be fine."

"YOU MUST BE wondering why I've called you here," Principal Jones said when Jolie entered her office that afternoon. "I received a rather disturbing phone call this morning."

I'm sure you did, Jolie thought, but she kept her thoughts to herself. Principal Jones was one of those administrators always concerned with how things appeared, especially to the public. While she supported her teachers, Jolie knew that other administrators in the district did a better job. However, her principal's shortcomings weren't enough for Jolie to request a transfer to a different school. Jolie folded her hands in her lap while Principal Jones settled behind the desk.

"So, answer me straight—did you have a date with Hank Friesen?"

Jolie refrained from rolling her eyes heavenward. "If you call going to Chuck E. Cheese's to discuss the possibility of tutoring his children a date."

"So you weren't out with him?"

"Not in the way you're insinuating," Jolie said. The thing about having a former school-district superintendent for a father was she knew how to control the conversation in situations like this. "Mr. Friesen was late picking up the children from latchkey, so he called me. By the time he arrived, they were starving. I agreed to accompany them to the restaurant so he and I could discuss the children's well-being. I drove my own car. If he and I were going out romantically, I certainly wouldn't go to a pizza place with a singing bear and loud music. I mean, would you?"

Principal Jones leaned back, laced her fingers together and studied Jolie. "I guess not," she conceded finally.

"Exactly. I'm sure if you ask your source—" Jolie deliberately paused for emphasis "—for more detailed information, you'd find out there was no kissing, hugging or touching of any kind. Nothing inappropriate. Just two people talking."

"Still—"

Jolie played her ace in the hole. "You're forgetting I'm a twin. Hank Friesen has twins who are in school for the first time. Who better to talk to about the challenges he's facing? He's not been here long enough to know that many people aside from those he works with."

"Oh," the principal said.

Jolie nodded. "Exactly. So perfectly innocent. Besides, you know I'm seeing someone." Okay, maybe not anymore, but her boss didn't know that.

"Fine," Principal Jones said, releasing her fingers. Now that she'd heard Jolie's side, she had better things to do. "If it's all professional, then I don't have a problem with your seeing him."

"I'm simply helping someone out," Jolie said. She was known for that and the principal nodded.

"Okay, then. As long as that's all it is."

As she'd told Carrie earlier, she knew where to draw the line. Jolie rose to her feet, ending the meeting. "If there's nothing else?"

"No, no," Principal Jones said, her hand already reaching for her mouse so she could check her e-mail.

Irritated that she'd been called to the principal's office, but reveling in her victory, Jolie smiled slightly to herself as she turned the knob and opened the door.

"SO THAT'S WHY I kept getting this problem wrong," Ethan said, grinning as the mathematical concept he'd been struggling with became clear. He worked another problem, getting it correct the first time. "I've got it!"

"You have," Jolie said, her smile wide. She gave Ethan a high five. Nothing was as cool as seeing a student suddenly grasp what you'd been trying to teach. "So do you think you can get the rest of that sheet done by yourself?"

"Yeah," Ethan said, taking his pencil to the next problem.

Jolie stood and moved to where Alli sat working on her history homework. "How are you doing?" Alli had had trouble in class today and Carrie had asked if Jolie wouldn't mind helping Alli review. Since she still tutored Ethan in math, Jolie'd agreed.

"Fine," Alli said, finishing matching the capital cities to their respective states. "I learned this with Grandma."

"It's still good practice to review. On the last test you only had thirty correct. That's sixty percent. I know you can score twenty percent higher."

"That's eighty percent," Alli said.

"Exactly," Jolie encouraged. "I bet if you practice even more you can be twenty percent higher than that."

"One hundred percent!" Alli exclaimed. She attacked the worksheet. "The capital of Missouri is Jefferson City. The capital of Illinois is Springfield. The…"

Jolie smiled to herself. The twins were doing much better academically and socially. While they worked, Jolie graded a few more papers. About ten minutes later her phone rang. A glance at the display revealed that the call came from the Graham Nolter. She picked it up. "Jolie Tomlinson."

"It's Hank."

"Hey." She hadn't spoken to him in over two weeks and she found herself warming to the sound of his voice. Sure, they'd e-mailed back and forth about how Ethan was doing, but she hadn't seen the man since that night at Chuck E. Cheese's. She told herself it was for the best. She didn't need any more meetings with the principal.

"I'm glad I caught you. I'll be blunt and come right out and say it. I need a favor. I'm sure I've already trod on your good graces enough, but if you could spare me one more, I'd be in your debt."

"What's up?" Jolie asked.

"I'm in the middle of a meeting that started much later than it was supposed to. We're on a five-minute break now, but this thing is going to last at least another two hours. You'd think planning fall-accommodation specials would go quickly, but that's not turning out to be the case. Would you mind driving Ethan and Alli back to the hotel? I'll be happy to give you gas money."

"Payment's not necessary," Jolie said. She glanced at the clock. A little after five. Normally she brought the children back to latchkey around five-thirty. Tonight she'd just take them home.

"I've asked the front desk to arrange for Elsa to come and babysit. I haven't had confirmation yet, but I expect to know something solid before you drop off the kids."

"That's fine. We're finishing up here and we'll be on our way soon."

"Thank you." She could hear the relief in his voice.

"Anytime," Jolie replied, meaning it. She liked Hank's kids a great deal. She liked him.

She set the phone down and tried to banish all thoughts of Hank's mischievous smile and broad shoulders. She reviewed Ethan's math problems and checked Alli's capital worksheet. "Okay, you two, good job. That's enough for today. Let's pack up. I'm going to be taking you home."

Ethan paused while placing his pencil inside his desk. "Dad's not coming?"

Jolie shook her head. "He's stuck in a meeting, so instead of taking you back to latchkey, I'll drop you off at the hotel. He said he called Elsa."

"He's always got a meeting." Alli sighed.

"Well, the work your dad does is very important," Jolie said, moving a few things around on her desk so she'd be prepared first thing in the morning.

"I guess. He is in charge of the whole place."

"Exactly," Jolie said, relieved Alli had become more accepting of her dad's job and the demands it made on his time. Jolie finished her next-day prep and grabbed her purse.

Alli had her backpack ready and Ethan finished zipping his closed. He glanced up expectantly.

"So we don't have to sign out with latchkey?" he asked.

"We'll walk by there and tell them you're going home with me. But let me warn you, my car's not as fancy as your dad's."

"His car came with the job," Ethan announced, slinging his backpack over one shoulder. "In Chicago, Dad would take the train to work. We lived in the suburbs."

"Well, my car's old, but it's paid for, so no complaints. It's even clean. I had it washed this weekend."

"The valets at the hotel do that for long-term guests. We could have yours done while you're there," Ethan said.

"No, that's not necessary." Jolie gave Ethan a wry smile. If he'd been her son, she'd have ruffled his hair. Boy, Hank certainly had some of life's small details wrapped up. A few minutes later Jolie had both kids buckled into the backseat and they were on their way.

"Is Chicago traffic this bad?" Jolie asked as she took one of the alternative routes through the city. Unlike getting to several other resorts located around Branson, reaching the 150-acre Nolter resort required a drive through town.

Traffic would become even more of a nightmare once the summer tourist season began. Then, weekend boaters, amusement-park goers and other vacationers just wanting to experience Branson's multitude of theaters would pack the strip and turn it into a parking lot. Coupled with the three lakes nearby, Branson was a vacationers' paradise.

A native to the constant gridlock, Jolie knew a few off-the-beaten-trail shortcuts and soon drove under the hotel portico. "I better come up and make sure Elsa's here," Jolie said, putting the car in Park.

"You can see my room," Alli suggested. The valet had

opened the rear door of the car, and he greeted the children as they climbed out. "This is Ms. Tomlinson, my teacher," Alli said as another valet helped Jolie out. "Please take care of her car. It's on me."

Jolie smiled at the assertion, but the valet regarded Alli in all seriousness. "Yes, Miss Friesen. Do you need me to take your backpack up to your room for you?"

"Oh, thanks, but I got it," Alli said. Jolie could tell the verbal exchange was a little game they played. Alli started off for the revolving doors, pausing as she reached them.

Jolie took the receipt from the younger valet and followed the children. Ethan had caught up with his sister and they each entered their own partition of the revolving automatic doors.

She'd been in the lobby of the Graham Nolter once before and, as it had then, the massive space awed her. A fountain in the center shot up two stories and cascaded down into a basin that became a bubbling brook. Lush foliage graced the entire space, which was lit by hidden lighting and skylights far above.

"We cross the brook to get to the east wing," Alli directed. "There's this bridge or that ramp over there— it's flatter for wheelchairs."

"You're quite the tour guide," Jolie said as they crossed the arched bridge and strolled down a path that led to the elevators. Alli was a contradiction. While in some ways she was far too mature for her age, as her precocious conversation with the valet had shown, in other ways her actions were more akin to an eight-year-old's than a ten-year-old's. Not that Alli was a slow learner or anything like that. But she often lacked emotional security and craved approval.

Alli pushed the button for the elevator, and once inside, Ethan pushed the button for the fifteenth floor. "We take turns," Ethan volunteered to Jolie's unanswered question. "Grandma taught us."

"That way we don't fight," Alli finished.

"That's very wise of your grandma," Jolie remarked. The doors opened and Alli fished a key card from her backpack. They made a right out of the elevator, and then a left. Jolie noticed that unlike a regular hotel floor, there were very few doors in this hallway. Alli led the way down the hall toward the last door. She pointed at one they passed.

"That room's Mrs. Drew's. She's lived here for five years. She's retired," Alli said.

"I wouldn't mind retiring here," Jolie said as she stepped into the Friesen suite. The suite was unlike any hotel room Jolie had ever stayed in. It occupied the entire corner of the building, offering a floor-to-ceiling panoramic view of the lake and the Nolter's golf course. Being on the top floor, it had higher-than-normal ceilings. There were several seating areas, a few pieces of sculpture and even a baby-grand piano.

"Do you play?" Jolie asked, noting that Elsa didn't appear to be waiting in the suite.

"I did when we lived in Chicago," Alli said. "That piano was my mom's. I haven't found a teacher here yet."

"So you want to keep playing?" Jolie asked.

Alli hung her book bag on a peg near the gourmet kitchen. "Uh-huh."

Jolie walked over and pressed a few keys. The notes flowed into the room; the piano was in perfect tune.

"Do *you* play?" Alli asked.

"I had a few lessons long ago. I'm not very good. My brother got all the musical talent."

"I still practice," Alli said, taking a seat on the black leather bench. She began to play a few notes of a more complicated piece. Jolie glanced around and saw that Ethan had hung his backpack up. As he wasn't nearby, she assumed he'd taken off for his bedroom. She'd check on him in a minute.

"That's very good," Jolie said when Alli lifted her hands from the keys.

"I'm not as good as my mom yet. She played with the symphony. Before me and Ethan came along."

"Ethan and I," Jolie corrected automatically. "I'm sure your mother is very proud that you're playing so well. You're better than I was at your age and my mom's a piano teacher."

"Wow." Alli soaked in the information. "Can she give me lessons?"

"We'll have to talk about it with your dad. Right now I need to find out what's happened to Elsa and check on your brother."

"Our rooms are through that door over there." Alli pointed to an open doorway. Behind it Jolie could see a small hallway. "Follow me and I'll show you my new American Girl doll. I got it from Grandmother and Grandfather. They said I can pick out a whole bunch of clothes for her when I visit Chicago this summer."

"That sounds wonderful. Let me check on your brother and then I'll be right in." Jolie paused outside the door on her left. It was ajar, so she knocked and pushed it slightly more open. "You in here, Ethan?"

"Yeah," he called.

"May I come in?"

"Yeah," he replied. Jolie opened the door and stepped through. Ethan's bedroom, the size of an average hotel room, had been customized. He had bunk beds, a seating area with a couch and a television hooked up to several game systems. The room was filled with toys and decorated with model airplanes. A guitar waited in a holder, and nearby on a music stand an open book displayed the song he'd practiced last. The computer on his desk kicked into screen-saver mode and began a slide show of rock bands. Ethan had plopped himself down on a beanbag chair and was playing a video game.

"You play guitar?"

"Yeah, a little. I'll practice later, after dinner."

"Would Elsa cook you dinner?"

He shook his head. "Nah. We'll order room service. We rarely use the kitchen. It's easier to just have the food brought up. Dad says we have an account."

"Ah," Jolie said. "Do you know how I could get hold of Elsa?"

"Front desk," Ethan answered, his gaze never wavering from the television screen.

"So you're fine in here by yourself?" she prodded.

"Uh-huh."

"Ms. Tomlinson? Are you coming?" Alli called.

"I'll be right there," Jolie said. It bothered her that Ethan had immediately disappeared and thrown himself into a video game. She left the room and crossed the hall to see Alli.

Where Ethan's room was all boy, Alli's was all girl. Everything was pink and white. Like Ethan she had a television and a computer, but much of her room was devoted to various brands of dolls and the houses and accessories that went with them. Alli was already holding up her newest American Girl doll, the latest limited-time model only out for the current year.

"This is Veronica," Alli said, displaying the doll. "I've already read her books."

"She's lovely." Jolie smiled. The doll really was beautiful. "I'm going to check on Elsa," she said, wandering into the suite's main living area. She found the phone and dialed zero for the operator.

"Front desk. This is Camille. How may I help you?"

Jolie quickly explained the situation and within a minute Camille was back on the line. "Elsa's on vacation this week."

Great, Jolie thought. She glanced at her watch. Surely Hank didn't plan to be gone all night.

"Do you want me to find someone else? I could transfer you to my manager," Camille offered.

"No, we're fine," Jolie replied, setting the phone down. She had Hank's cell number and could always call him. She decided against that idea. Obviously the meeting was important or he wouldn't have contacted her in the first place.

"Ms. Tomlinson," Ethan called, entering the room. "I'm hungry."

Jolie's stomach chose that moment to growl.

"Can we get room service now?" Ethan asked. "There's a button on the phone that goes right to the kitchen."

"I guess ordering dinner would be a good idea," Jolie said.

"The menu is in that desk drawer." Ethan pointed.

"Will you please get it for me?" Jolie asked. Ethan retrieved the menu and she flipped it open. "What does your sister eat?"

Ethan shrugged. "I don't know."

"I'd better go ask her," Jolie said. "You pick something out."

"Elsa usually gets the steak. You should probably order her one," Ethan suggested as Jolie reached the doorway to the hall.

She turned around. "Elsa's on vacation. She's not coming tonight. I'm staying until your dad gets in."

Ethan didn't seem too upset and, in fact, issued a genial "Cool" before opening up the menu. "Can I order two things, then?"

"*May* I," Jolie corrected, "and it depends on what they are."

"Rats," she heard him say, and she smiled to herself as she knocked on Alli's door.

"Come in," Alli said.

"Hey." Jolie pushed the door open and stepped into the room. "Ethan and I are going to order dinner from room service. What would you like?"

Alli's eyebrows rose. "Elsa's not coming?"

"She's on vacation. I guess your dad didn't know. I'm staying until he gets back. I'd cook something, but your brother says you always order in."

"Sometimes we go downstairs to the restaurant, but not very much. If Dad's downstairs people like to talk to him and he always stops and talks for a long time. It's boring." She'd changed her doll into a new outfit and she fingered the fringed hem.

"The menu's in the living room. Why don't you come with me and pick something?"

"Can I order off the adult menu? I'm tired of chicken strips."

"Yes, you *may,*" Jolie said, "as long as it's not too unreasonable. No fifty-dollar steaks or anything like that."

"I want the catfish. Elsa's had it and it comes with mashed potatoes and those really thin green beans. And dinner rolls. I like those. Dad always orders extras just for me."

"I think that sounds fine," Jolie replied, leaving Alli and returning to Ethan. When told he could eat off the adult menu, too, he ordered fried chicken. Jolie opted for a salad topped with beef tenderloin and about a half hour later their meal arrived.

"Hey, Anton," Alli said, skipping into the room as Anton wheeled in the room-service cart.

"Hi there, Alli." Anton's gap-toothed smile widened as the girl gazed at the silver-domed trays. "I see you've given up kids' food."

"We both have," Ethan said. "We're ten now. We'll be eleven in September."

"Do you want it on the dining-room table or do you want to grab it like usual?" Anton asked.

Ethan and Alli glanced at each other and then Jolie, who knew just eating dinner at a table together was one of the most important things a family could do.

"We always ate together when I was growing up," she told them. "We'll eat in here tonight."

"Table it is," Anton said, moving the contents of the cart to the appropriate places on the table. He set Jolie's salad at the head. "Miss."

Alli giggled at that. "This is Ms. Tomlinson. She's our teacher."

"And a very fine one at that, I'm sure," Anton said without missing a beat. He'd finished distributing the food and was moving his cart out of the way.

"Do I need to sign anything?" Jolie asked, looking for the bill.

"Oh, no," Anton said. "We've already put everything on Mr. Friesen's account. I'll show myself out. Call down when you want the dishes removed and someone will be right up. Just leave everything where it is."

"Oh, okay, thank you." Jolie said, gesturing for the children to take their seats. Everything appeared delicious, especially the kids' mashed potatoes, which were made from small red potatoes with the skin left on. Jolie was a sucker for potatoes.

"So tell me about your day," Jolie said to the twins. That was the question her mother had always used and it seemed a good place to start tonight.

"It was fine," Alli said, her grandmother-taught manners evident as she cut her catfish.

"I liked the assembly," Jolie prodded, cutting her steak and mixing it in with the salad.

"Yeah, the magician was pretty cool. I liked when he made his top hat disappear," Ethan said.

But Alli remained quiet.

"What about you?" Jolie asked her.

Alli swallowed and shook her head. "I don't usually talk during dinner," she said.

"Why not?" Jolie asked.

"Elsa lets us watch TV, instead."

Jolie frowned. "Well, we're not going to do that tonight. When I was growing up one of my favorite times was dinner. My brothers and sisters told stories and we laughed a lot."

"We just watch celebrity-news shows," Ethan inserted.

"Which are rubbish." Jolie didn't care what movie star was in rehab. "So, Alli, did you like the magic show?"

"It was okay," she said, shoveling a huge forkful of food into her mouth, letting those manners she'd been using earlier slip.

"I thought it was great," Ethan argued. "I don't know how you think it was just okay."

Jolie smiled ruefully as Ethan began to dominate the conversation. At least someone was talking, although she did have to remind him to wipe his mouth twice and to close it when chewing.

Dinner ended a little after seven. "Do you shower in the a.m. or p.m.?" Jolie asked.

"I'm a.m. and he's p.m.," Alli said.

"When's bedtime?" Jolie asked, although she remembered what Hank had told her at Chuck E. Cheese's.

The twins glanced at each other as if trying to send a telepathic message.

"Truthfully," Jolie warned.

"We have to be in bed at eight-thirty with lights-out at nine. We can read for a half hour," Ethan answered.

"Then we'd best get moving," Jolie said. "I assume you both can do the bathroom thing yourselves."

"Yep," they said in unison.

"Then get to it. When you're in your pajamas, come out here with me."

Pretty soon all three sat on the couch as they viewed one of the latest Disney Channel programs. By eight thirty-five, Jolie had them in bed, teeth brushed and clothes ready for tomorrow.

She left them in their rooms and headed out to the living area. She retrieved her cell phone from her purse and pressed a button, bringing the screen to life, but there were no calls. She scrolled down to find Hank's number and dialed. She could hear a phone ringing and looked over her shoulder to see Hank walking through the door. She ended the call and watched as Hank tried to balance his briefcase, overcoat and cell phone.

"Your missed call is me," she told him.

"Jolie!" He was so surprised he lost control of the bundle in his arms. His briefcase hit the floor with a thud and came to rest on its side. He caught his cell, but the overcoat puddled at his feet. "Sorry. You surprised me. I didn't expect to see you. Where's Elsa?"

"She's apparently on vacation," Jolie said. "She wasn't here when we arrived, so I checked with the front desk."

His face whitened. "No one told me. I'm so sorry. I didn't intend for you to stay with them."

"They weren't any trouble," she said.

He picked up his briefcase and placed it on the foyer table. He moved his coat to the closet. "It doesn't matter that they weren't any trouble, although I'm glad they behaved. You're their teacher. I never intended..." He paused, looking stricken.

Jolie touched his arm. Her fingers noted the smooth texture of the suit's high-quality material. "It's fine. Relax. Both of them are in bed. Why don't you see them before lights-out?"

His shoulders dropped slightly, but he still seemed nervous. "Would you mind waiting until I say good-night to my kids before you leave? I know I shouldn't keep you any longer, but I'd like to talk with you if you can spare a moment."

She'd planned on bolting for the door the minute he arrived, using an excuse such as grading papers or even saying she needed to do laundry. Yet something about the way he looked at her made her want to stay.

"It's fine," she said. "I'll be here."

Chapter Six

"And she even let us eat off the adult menu," Alli announced as her father tucked her into bed. "I ate almost everything. There's a little bit left. She found some containers and put everything in those. They're in the fridge. That way I can reheat it tomorrow."

"Sounds like a plan," Hank said, marveling at how well Jolie had handled his kids. He'd tucked Ethan in first and his son had sung Jolie's praises, too. He adjusted his daughter's covers and turned off the lamp, the only glow in the room coming from her princess night-light. "I love you, honey," he said, leaning over to kiss Alli's forehead.

She arched upward and wrapped her arms around his neck. "Love you, too, Dad."

Hank felt a little tug on his heart as she ended the contact and nestled down to sleep. It was in moments like this he thought of Amanda. The longing for what should have been didn't come as often as it had five years ago, but like a faded dream, occasionally he felt the bitter pang of profound loss. He'd moved on, but she would never be forgotten. She'd always been with him to do the bedtime routine. She'd smile at him, take his hand and lead him toward…

He shook the memory from his head. He had to let

Amanda go and focus on the here and now. He was determined to get his life back on track.

His boss, Peter, who'd lost his first wife years ago and happily remarried, had been giving Hank subtle hints that maybe it was time he started dating again. In his late sixties and beginning to make retirement noises, Peter had been married to his second wife, Claire, for twenty years. It had been Peter who'd spurred on Hank to apply for and accept the Nolter job. The change of scenery seemed to be doing his kids a world of good. The signs were small, but positive. And most of them could be directly attributed to the very special woman waiting for him out in the living room.

"Are they down for the night?" she asked when he returned.

He nodded, finding it odd to discover he had a lump in his throat. "Yes," he replied, indulging in a brief cough to retrieve his voice. "Thank you. I had no idea Elsa was on vacation. I guess I delegated too much and tonight things got messed up."

"It happens," Jolie said. She'd risen from her spot on the couch and they stood there awkwardly, almost nose to nose.

Hank gestured to the couch, suddenly anxious. He didn't want her to leave. "Do you have a few minutes?"

Jolie sat back down. Outside the world was dark and he could see her reflection in one of the huge windows. Her eyes were the most interesting shade of green. Not quite emerald, but nowhere close to being blue.

He shouldn't be staring at her face. Her lips had parted slightly as if she was anticipating something. She wore no lipstick, but her lips were naturally full and pink. He had the urge to kiss her.

"This is a bit awkward for me," he admitted, sitting in a chair about six feet from her and trying to regain control of his libido. "I've never had to ask this type of favor from anyone. You're their teacher. It's like asking a doctor for a free medical exam because you know him slightly. Rather unprofessional."

"It happens," Jolie said. She didn't appear upset and Hank relaxed. "My brother Clay's a foot doctor. Everyone at parties tells him their medical problems."

"That doesn't make it right. You shouldn't have had to babysit my children," Hank insisted. She blinked. He found her eyes a bit hypnotic. Perhaps Peter was right—Hank needed to date. But could he ask Jolie out? He wanted to. Maybe in June once school was out? Jolie was speaking and Hank focused on what she was saying.

"I figured it was best to just stay. If I'd called you, your meeting would have been interrupted, making it last longer once you'd gotten restarted. You'd be stressed, and who needs that?"

He smiled wryly at her assessment. "You've nailed it. That's a bit scary. You're not going to tell me I'm like this because I'm a man, are you?"

She grinned. Her shoulders didn't seem as tense and her laughter bubbled out light and upbeat. "Are you telling me you're not a typical man?"

"Oh, I'm sure I am. I just don't want to hear it. It'll deflate my oversize ego."

"My twin brother has one of those."

"I keep forgetting you're a twin."

She nodded, and her hair loosened from its clip. She took the clip out, letting the brownish-red locks fall to her shoulders. "I wear it up for work," she said, a slight flush creeping up her neck. Hank's palms started to sweat.

"You're not at work," he responded, surprised at the huskiness of his voice. Was he flirting? Did he even remember how?

"I'm sorry if that sounded inappropriate," he apologized,

deciding to stop any silliness before it led somewhere unexpected. "Obviously you're not at work."

Her demeanor didn't change. "I understood what you meant. It was fine. Like I told you before, we can be friends. I grew up with one sister and three brothers. I can dish it out as well as I can take it, which, let me tell you, can be pretty scary when all five of us are together and the fur begins to fly."

She might have told him that at Chuck E. Cheese's, but if she had, her words hadn't registered. He'd listened and found her fascinating, but he hadn't taken any of her offers of friendship or babysitting seriously. He'd thought she was simply being polite. Now he knew differently, which raised her even higher in his esteem. "So you're close?" he asked.

"Very. We all live within a half-hour drive of each other, including my parents, so we get together often. My nieces and nephews are plentiful and so are my cousins, and there's always something to celebrate in my family, whether it's a birthday, a baby shower or someone's anniversary."

"I wish I could spend more time with my family," he said. "I've seen my parents once since I arrived back and they live in Springfield, less than an hour away. The kids still haven't visited. We usually only get to see my parents during the holidays."

"Well, perhaps you'll see them more now that you're living in Missouri," Jolie said.

"I hope so. I have to admit, I really relied on Amanda's parents after her death. I realized one day that Ethan and Alli ran to them, instead of me. It was quite a wake-up call. I didn't like it one bit."

He hadn't planned to share such intimate information, but the way Jolie listened without judging him made his tongue loose. She nodded and replied, "Then you made a wise choice to break free."

Her comment warmed his soul. He'd wrestled long and hard with the decision to move and take Alli and Ethan away from daily contact with their maternal grandparents. "I thought so. It's still difficult."

"Don't worry, you'll settle in. You've only been here a month. You'll have all summer to spend together. School's out in two weeks."

"Although then I'll be faced with a dilemma I've never had before. Child care. The twins aren't old enough to stay home by themselves, but they're too old to be in a traditional center. We have a Kids' Day Out program, which is a full day of supervised activities for kids. But I'd rather not have my children mingling too much with the vacationing hotel guests. That could get awkward if there are problems. I've enrolled them in the summer enrichment program, but that only covers June."

"What about day camps or options like that?" Jolie suggested. "Parks and Recreation has a great program."

"Good idea. I hadn't thought about that and I'll check into it. See, I'm lost with this stuff. Amanda would have known, or at least her mother would have. In fact, Sylvia wants them to visit for the entire month of July, but I told her no. We need time to become a family."

"I'm guessing she probably wasn't too happy about that."

Hank shook his head. She'd been quite upset. The conversation had been heated and included Sylvia telling him he was ruining his children's lives. Hank grimaced. "She wasn't pleased, but I have to believe this is for the best."

"You're their dad," Jolie stated, as if that made everything all right. The matter-of-fact way she said it touched him.

He smiled wistfully. "Yeah, but what if I'm wrong? What if the best thing for my kids is to be raised by their grandparents? What if I'm such a lousy parent I'm doing more harm than good?"

Her face paled and Hank glimpsed a rare moment of sadness and vulnerability in her eyes. She moved to sit near him as if her proximity could somehow vanquish the demons he battled. "That's simply not possible. You may not believe it, but you have to hold fast to the tenet that you are the best person for the job. No matter what the twins' grandmother says."

"I..." Her presence was a comfort. She'd balanced on the edge of the chair and he pulled her close. He wanted to hold her, to feel her goodness next to him. He wanted to get his fingers into her hair and his lips on hers. She was a balm to his soul—she made him feel alive again.

She was a woman and he was a man. And after five long years, he was finally ready to act on that fact. As for Jolie, she looked almost expectant, as if she wanted exactly what he did.

"Dad?"

Hank released Jolie instantly, and turned to face his daughter. Alli stood in the doorway, rubbing her eyes. She stepped into the room. "I had a bad dream."

"Come here, sweetie," Hank said, and his daughter picked up her pace and threw herself into his arms for a reassuring hug.

"Do you want to tell me about it?" Hank asked.

"I don't remember it. Just that it was scary," Alli said. She turned her face so that she could see Jolie. "Hi, Ms. Tomlinson," she said shyly.

"I think you should probably call me Jolie when we're not at school," Jolie suggested.

"Okay."

Hank loosened his grip on his daughter as she turned to fully face Jolie, but he still felt his arms around her.

"So a bad dream, huh?" Jolie asked.

Alli nodded, eyes wide. "Monsters were trying to get me."

Jolie smiled reassuringly. "Have you been watching any Goosebumps videos?"

"Yesterday," Alli admitted.

"What are those?" Hank asked, thinking he should get rid of them immediately.

"Scary stories for kids. R. L. Stine wrote the book series," Jolie informed him. She focused her attention on Alli. "The stories aren't true. But your brain works while you sleep. It's still processing those images, which is why you're having dreams. You can control your dreams. Just have your brain tell itself to wake up."

"Can it do that?" Alli's eyes widened even more.

"It can." Jolie touched Alli's forehead. "The power to stop them is right here. Adults have bad dreams, too. But we can learn to control them. We can direct the movie in our head."

Hank thought about that. Certainly there were times when bad dreams snagged him and didn't let go until he woke up shaking, but the ones where someone chased him with a chain saw? He was always the victor in that one.

"What Jolie says is true. I use the technique myself," he said. He gave Alli a little squeeze and she wriggled a bit in his arms. She also yawned, signaling that it was the perfect time to put her back to bed.

"Let's go, sleepyhead. Next time, have your brain yell, 'Wake up!' or 'This is only a dream!' It should work," Hank said.

"I'll try," Alli promised. Hank stood and swung her into his arms. She weighed about eighty-five pounds, but he carried her easily and soon had her tucked back into bed.

"I love you," Alli said, her eyes already closed and sleep taking over as he kissed her one last time. When he returned to the living area, Jolie was already on her feet, her purse slung over her shoulder.

"It's getting late. I need to go," she told him.

As much as he'd enjoyed talking to her, he realized that she was right. "Thank you again," he said, making sure not to get too close. He didn't entirely trust himself around her.

"If you need my help again, don't hesitate to call. I don't expect anything in return."

He almost wished she did. He'd never met anyone who didn't want something from him. The idea of having a friend who was a woman and not a business colleague was a foreign concept to Hank.

He'd had female friends in high school, but that was more than twenty-five years ago. When he'd been married to Amanda, she'd been his best friend. He'd kept all other female relationships friendly yet impersonal. He wanted to be very personal with Jolie.

Jolie strode to the foyer, and he followed at a respectable distance. She pressed down on the door handle and Hank moved forward then so he could hold the door open for her. "Thank you. I can't say it enough," he said. His face was about eighteen inches from hers. He inhaled the light floral fragrance she wore.

The right corners of her lips inched upward. "I like your kids."

"And me?" The two words seemed to come out on their own volition. He didn't want to be friends. He wanted to kiss her.

"You have enough on your plate," she said. "Keep things simple. *Friends.*" Then she stepped out of the suite and proceeded down the hall. He leaned out and watched her until she rounded the corner. She didn't glance back once.

JOLIE PRESSED the button for the lobby and slowly exhaled. She hadn't realized she'd been holding her breath. Man, did Hank's presence rattle her. What would have happened had Alli not interrupted? And there at the door, when he'd been so near…

She'd wanted to kiss him. She'd imagined it in her dreams, fantasized how his lips would feel on hers. Not only did she find him incredibly attractive, she liked him a great deal. He was a man who valued family and hard work, two things very important to her. He impressed her.

Which was the problem. She couldn't give in to the pheromones. Or hormones. Or whatever it was that caused her to feel light-headed and giddy whenever she was around the man.

She was single and…well, so was Hank. But he was the parent of one of her students. That was a big issue, especially since he was the most interesting man she'd met in ages. And she certainly didn't want to be alone for the rest of her life.

She sighed and jabbed the down button again. Dating in your thirties was horrible. Either you invested yourself in something only to be burned, or you simply didn't make the relationship a priority and things just fizzled. That's what had happened with her and Chad.

She resisted the urge to stomp her foot. Where was that elevator? Taking its own sweet time, obviously. She tried to calm her nerves. As she'd told Carrie, she knew how to draw the line.

But she empathized with Hank. She understood the guilt that accompanied terrible loss. It took time to rebuild and Hank was only getting started.

Chapter Seven

Jolie's phone rang the next morning before school started. She glanced at the caller ID, which revealed the early-morning call was coming from the Graham Nolter resort. Her fingertips hovered over the phone, and moments before it went to voice mail she snatched the receiver. "Hello."

"Hi. It's Hank."

His deep voice washed over her, a reminder she'd spent a sleepless night thinking of him. He'd haunted her, and her frustration at being unable to date or touch him had had her tossing and turning.

"Are you there?" he asked.

"Yes, sorry," she replied, determined to get it together.

"I wanted to apologize if I was out of line at any time last night," he said.

"You were fine."

"Good." He paused a moment. "I didn't want to be."

She gripped the phone tighter. "No?"

"No. I'd very much like to ask you out. Just you and me."

"We could meet to discuss the kids," she replied.

"That's not what I meant."

"I'm their teacher," she protested. She checked the clock. One minute before she had to go get her class from the gym and start school.

"I understand. Let me know if you change your mind."

"I can't." Although she wanted to do just that.

"School's out in two weeks. I'll try again then."

"Really, I—" The bell rang. Her clock must be off. "I have to go get my class."

"Have a good day," Hank said.

Jolie set the phone down. She left the room, almost bumping into Carrie.

"Hey, what's wrong?" her friend asked.

"Nothing," Jolie said. The principal supervised at the end of the hallway, watching as the kindergarteners filed out first. "Nothing."

"CAN YOU BELIEVE how the past two weeks flew by?" Carrie asked on the Friday before Memorial Day, the last day of school before summer vacation. The two teachers were eating lunch together as usual.

"Time went fast," Jolie agreed, enjoying the peace and quiet of the half day. The students had already been dismissed and, except for those in the latchkey program, they'd all gone home.

"So will you continue tutoring the Friesen twins over the summer as you did after school?" Carrie asked.

"I don't think so," Jolie replied, glancing around her classroom. She'd removed everything from the walls and the place was pretty bare. "They're all caught up and ready for fifth grade. My time as their teacher is done."

"That could be a good thing." Carrie waved her plastic fork.

"Why's that?" Jolie stared at her lunch. She'd made macaroni-and-cheese last night and hadn't reheated the leftovers long enough in the faculty-lounge microwave. Already the noodles were tepid and tasteless.

"Well, you and their dad seem to be getting along."

Jolie resisted the urge to look skyward. Ever since that early-morning call, Hank had backed off. "I told you he only needs a friend. I haven't seen him since the night I took Ethan and Alli home and, remember, nothing happened. We've talked on the phone, but only for him to ask me to give the kids a ride home. The few times I've dropped them off, Elsa has been there."

"Their babysitter." Carrie took a bite of her mixed-greens salad. As always, Carrie's lunch looked much more appealing.

"Yes. She's actually very nice. She's in her early twenties and hopes to perform on Broadway. She's singing in the lounge at the Nolter in hopes of getting transferred to their Manhattan hotel. If she gets on there, she'll have steady work while she auditions."

"She sounds young and beautiful," Carrie said, warning clear.

Jolie rolled her eyes. "She is. But she cares for the children. She's the oldest of a large family and she misses them dearly. They live in Joplin. Anyway, it's not like I'm after Hank."

"Why not? You aren't Ethan's teacher anymore. No conflict of interest."

Jolie frowned. As much as she hated to admit it, since that early-morning phone call she'd let herself fantasize all kinds of scenarios. "Yes, but what if we did date? It might be awkward for the kids to see me at school after things ended."

"Oh, please. The signs are clear—fate wants you to pursue this. The district even transferred Mrs. Jones to the middle school, so you won't have to worry about her being on your case."

"I think Hank has more important things to deal with than dating," Jolie protested. "As do I. Remember? I agreed to take Barbara's spot teaching summer school when she had to cancel. I was looking forward to some time off, but I couldn't resist the extra cash."

Like many other public districts across the state, Jolie's school would host a summer-school program. However, at the elementary buildings, the program focused on enrichment, not credit recovery. Thus, even top students often spent four more weeks in school, but this time studying everything from rocketry to robotics in addition to three hours of reading, writing and arithmetic. Jolie would be dropping down a level to teach a class of third graders.

"So when will you see him next?" Carrie asked.

"I don't know. I'm not worried about it. I've got the family picnic tomorrow. The big Tomlinson annual reunion. Already Dad's got campers all over the place as all our relatives climb out of the woodwork for the holiday weekend."

Carrie made a face. "I like families, but yours is insane."

"They are when they all get together and there are way too many to keep track of." Jolie covered her macaroni-and-cheese container. Despite the lackluster taste, she'd eaten it all. "I guess we'd better get going. I have a few things left to do before checkout."

Teacher checkout was fairly simple, and involved turning in room keys and some necessary paperwork.

"I'm finished," Carrie announced, packing up her lunch containers.

Jolie snorted in disbelief. "You sicken me. I still have to print out my grade reports."

"Not me. I'm getting out of here so I can finish packing. Tomorrow we're leaving to see Brian's family in Sacramento."

"Ah, that's right," Jolie said.

"It's always a long drive and equally long visit when we return to our hometown. Don't stay too late today."

"I won't. Hank asked me to drop off the kids and I promised Ethan and Alli I'd get them by two. They want to go swimming."

"You should just marry Hank and be done with it. You're like a mom to those kids already," Carrie said.

"Am not," Jolie replied, but the thought nagged at her for the next hour as she worked on getting her checkout materials together.

"SO WILL WE SEE you again?" Alli asked later that afternoon as they pulled up in front of the Nolter.

"We'll see her in summer school," Ethan told his sister.

"Right. It starts the Monday after next. I'll be there," Jolie confirmed.

Alli pouted. "I don't want to stay with Elsa all next week. I want to stay with you. My dad could pay you."

"Don't be a baby, Alli. Dad says Jolie's a teacher, not a babysitter," Ethan scoffed as he climbed out of the car. He slammed the door behind him before the valet could close it, and Jolie winced at the harsh thud.

"You're not a baby and I'm no longer your brother's teacher," Jolie told Alli. "Since school's out, you can consider me your friend. Your dad has my number and you can call me if you want."

Alli's pout disappeared and was replaced with a bright smile. "Okay. Maybe you can come swimming!"

"That's the spirit," Jolie said.

"Are you coming, Alli?" Elsa called from the hotel entrance, and Alli climbed out of the car.

She reluctantly grabbed her art portfolio and her backpack. "Bye."

"Bye. You take care," Jolie said. She waited until the kids were inside the hotel before she sighed and drove off. She was going to miss them. They'd grown on her since April. She'd tutored them, listened to them and decided that Hank had great kids. He'd done well. She frowned. After today she'd have no reason to talk to Hank. She didn't like that one bit.

Jolie exited the hotel grounds. She wasn't due at her parents' until later, so she drove toward home. A raw melancholy settled over her. It had to do with saying goodbye to her students, and also with the thought of never seeing Hank again. She also wasn't ready for this weekend, which commemorated one of the worst memories of her life—losing her child.

She'd done what the experts said: put Ruthie to sleep on her back on a firm mattress with nothing in the crib. Still, her child had become one of the approximately 2,500 that died of SIDS every year. There were simply no answers.

She tried to convince herself to let go of the sadness and celebrate summer. After all, she was on vacation! She was looking forward to doing some scrapbooking this week, she wanted to take a hike at one of the conservation areas, and she had a list of DVDs she wanted to watch.

Jolie turned into her apartment complex. She'd chosen this complex because it sat in the hills above the lake, and if she squinted hard enough when standing on her balcony, she could see a hint of blue down through the trees. The view was clearer in the winter. Her town house had only one bedroom, but it was in the loft overlooking the living area, which made the space airy and bright.

Her cell phone began to trill as she unlocked her door, and she managed to catch the call on the last ring, at the same time jockeying the door closed behind her.

"Jolie, it's Hank."

"Hi," she said as calmly as she could. There was no reason for her to act like a teenage girl upon hearing a boy's voice.

"Hey. I'm glad I caught you. I told you I'm at corporate headquarters in Chicago for a couple of days, didn't I?"

"You did," she replied. They'd talked briefly two nights ago when Ethan had had a question about his math homework.

"I've got a dilemma. I was scheduled on the 7:00 p.m. flight home, but corporate wants me at a dinner. It's a personal invitation from the CEO. I told my boss already that I might not be able to make it, but…"

She could tell from his voice how important it was that he attend. "Is there anything I can do to help?" she asked.

"I hate to impose on you again—you've done so much already… My parents have said they could stay with the kids, but they can't make it to the hotel until ten. Can you spot Elsa until they arrive? She has to be in the hotel lounge at seven."

"When are you coming back?"

"I'll be on the first flight out tomorrow. I have to connect in St. Louis, so around eleven."

"I have to be at my parents' tonight. It's our annual family-reunion weekend."

"Oh…I'm sorry. Of course, you need to be there. I'll call the front desk and—"

"If you'd like, I could take the twins with me. Many of my nieces and nephews are their age, so there'll be lots of kids for them to play with. While the reunion officially starts tomorrow morning, at least half the crowd arrived today and is camped out all over the place. Call your parents back and tell them I'll keep the twins. There's no sense in them stressing and trying to get down here. The highway is going to be packed enough."

Memorial Day weekend officially started the summer season. Highway 65 south of Springfield, even though four lanes, would be heavily traveled. "That's true," Hank admitted. "Will your parents mind?"

"Not at all. Mom has a huge upstairs sleeping porch that she lines with camp cots for all the girls. The boys will bunk in the barn. There's always plenty of room."

"Ethan would like that," Hank said.

"Do you have a pen and paper? I'll give you directions to my parents' place. You can pick up the twins there anytime tomorrow afternoon."

"Okay, I'm ready."

She dictated directions to the farm. "Could you let Elsa know I'll be picking up the kids? Tell her I'll meet them in the suite. I want to make sure they have the appropriate gear packed. My parents have a pool, so there'll be swimming. Do you mind if they ride the horses?"

"No, that would be fantastic. They'll love it!"

"Great. I promise they'll have a good time," she said, already making mental notes of items Ethan and Alli needed. "If you have any questions or changes, just call me. My phone will be on."

"Will do."

Jolie said a quick goodbye and hung up.

Less than forty minutes later—after packing her overnight case and stowing it in the trunk—she'd reached the hotel. The valet greeted her by name. "Nice to see you again, Ms. Tomlinson."

"I won't be here long. About a half hour, tops," she told him. She walked through the hotel entrance and got on the elevator.

Elsa opened the door to the suite and Jolie strode inside. "Hey, thanks for coming early."

"Not a problem. Are the kids in their rooms?"

"Yes. We never got to the pool."

"They can swim tonight," Jolie said.

"I'm sure they'll have a good time," Elsa said, grabbing her purse from the foyer table. "Thanks again." Elsa waved as she walked out the door and pulled it closed behind her.

Jolie went into the hallway where both kids' doors were shut and called, "Okay, who's up for swimming?"

"Jolie!" Alli reached her first and threw her arms around Jolie's waist. The hug tugged at something deep within Jolie, and she patted Alli on the back. "Hey, kiddo."

"Hi, Jolie." This from Ethan, who observed the scene from the doorway.

"Hi!" Jolie smiled. "You're going to have a great time on my parents' farm. We're having a family reunion, so there'll be tons of things to do both today and tomorrow. Do you have suitcases or duffel bags?"

Alli nodded. "Like what things?"

"Swimming. Horseback riding. Trampoline. Swings. Last time there was even one of those inflatable bounce houses."

Ethan's mouth dropped open. "You must have lots of space."

Jolie grinned. "One hundred acres that's been in my family for over a century. We live on about five. The rest is used for grazing cattle and growing corn. You'll need to bring a swimsuit, a beach towel, a change of clothes, pajamas and toiletries."

"What are those?" Alli asked.

"Toothbrush. Toothpaste. Hairbrush. Those things," Jolie answered. "You need to bring boots if you have them and a pair of jeans so you can ride. My dad's barbecuing tonight, so we'll eat dinner later. Did you have a snack?"

They nodded. About thirty minutes later both kids were packed and pulling wheeled duffel bags behind them.

Jolie loaded everything into her car and drove to her parents' house. She hadn't called first, so her mother looked a little shocked as she stepped out onto the side porch and saw Jolie pull into the parking area with two children in the back.

Her mother quickly regained her composure. She wiped her hands on her apron, walked down the steps and approached the car. "Hi, Jolie."

"Hi, Mom." Jolie climbed out. "This is Ethan Friesen and his twin, Alli. Ethan was a new student in my class at the end of the year. Their dad is in Chicago until tomorrow so I offered to bring the kids with me to help him out."

"Jolie was our tutor," Alli added helpfully. Both children were out of the car and standing next to Jolie.

"Ethan, Alli, this is my mother. She's also Mrs. Tomlinson, but everyone calls her either Maudie or Grandma Maudie."

"I like Maudie," Ethan replied. Then he remembered his manners. "It's nice to meet you, Maudie."

Jolie's mom smiled. "Glad you could come visit, Ethan. Most of the boys are down at the barn with Jolie's brother Bill. We just had a foal born last night."

"A baby horse! Can I see it, too?" Alli asked.

"A little later," Maudie said with a smile. "All the girls are in the pool, so if you want to swim, now's your best chance to swim without any boys present. Let's go introduce you to everyone, shall we?"

Jolie opened the trunk and took out the suitcases. "We're all staying the night," she said.

Her mother arched both eyebrows but said only, "Girls on the sunporch, boys in the barn loft like always. I have extra sleeping bags."

"I was counting on that," Jolie said, knowing she'd be subject to the third degree later. She'd worry about the inquisition then. At the moment she wanted to get the children settled in.

"So why are the girls and boys separated?" Alli asked as Maudie whistled for one of the older boys.

"It's easier that way sometimes," Maudie said. "Tomorrow everyone will be everywhere, but for today, the girls wanted the pool to themselves. The boys do far too many cannonballs."

"I can do those," Ethan said, watching as a boy of about thirteen approached.

"Avery, this is Ethan. He's your aunt Jolie's guest, so I expect all of you boys to show him proper hospitality. Make sure the other boys know that and tell them if they don't make him feel welcome, they'll deal with me."

"Yes, ma'am," Avery said to his grandmother, his long brown bangs slashed diagonally across his face.

"Why don't you show Ethan the foal and introduce him to Skip and Fred? They're about Ethan's age. Also, get him a bunk in the barn."

"Yes, ma'am," Avery repeated, and he reached for the duffel Jolie held out. Within seconds Ethan was off in the distance and entering the barn.

"Let's take your stuff upstairs and get you changed to swim," Jolie suggested to Alli. As a few toddlers raced by, parents in pursuit, Alli timidly reached for Jolie's hand.

"I'll leave you to it," Jolie's mom told her, and soon, they were in the house and headed up the back stairs to the sunporch.

The porch overlooked the backyard and the pool, which Jolie noticed contained at least eight girls around Alli's age. The high-school girls charged with lifeguarding sat around and soaked up the sun, occasionally getting in the water to cool off. The windows of the sunporch were open, letting in the breeze, and Alli could hear the laughter.

"We'll get you down there in a minute," Jolie said, setting Alli's duffel on a cot. "This will be where you sleep. I won't be too far away. My room's right through that door there. To get to the hall and the bathroom, you go through this door, the same one we came in."

"So your room is attached to the sunporch?"

"It is." Jolie opened the door so Alli could see. Her childhood bedroom had been redecorated, but it still contained the same wooden furniture and two twin beds. "My sister and I shared a room. We used to play out here all the time. Now my mom uses this for all the grandchildren."

"So you'll be right there."

"Yes." Alli appeared relieved and Jolie asked, "You've never been away at a sleepover before, have you?"

Alli shook her head, her blond hair swishing. "No."

"Then you'll love this. All the cots will be filled with girls your age. Let's grab your swimsuit and you can use my room to change. I'll wait outside."

While Alli was changing, Jolie's phone rang. "I had a few minutes before dinner. How's it going?" Hank asked.

"Great. We're here and Alli's on her way to the pool, where the girls have taken control. My mom put Ethan in Avery's capable hands—he's my brother Bill's son. I'll check on them later, but I'm sure Ethan's fine."

"Good," Hank said. "I really owe you one, Jolie. I keep saying that, don't I?"

"You do and I'll collect at some point. Alli's going to get her first sleepover tonight," Jolie said. "I didn't realize she'd never spent the night with friends."

"Neither did I," Hank admitted.

"She'll have a ball. My room is right next to where she'll be sleeping, so I'll be nearby if there are problems."

"That's good. I've got to run. Do you mind if I call you tonight? Talk to my kids?"

"They'd love that. Traditionally bedtime for the younger set is around ten."

"They'll be worn-out by then."

"That's sort of the point." Jolie laughed.

"I'll call before then," Hank said. He disconnected and Jolie put the phone in her jeans shorts as Alli came out in her very conservative one-piece.

"That's a pretty suit," Jolie said. It was only a little white lie.

"My grandma picked it out," Alli said. "I used it for swim lessons."

That explained it. Most of the other girls would be wearing bikinis. Jolie resolved to suggest to Hank that Alli buy one. Or even a one-piece in a floral or a fun, funky bright pattern.

"Your dad called. He's going to try to call you tonight."

Alli shrugged. "Sometimes he says he will and then he gets busy and can't."

Jolie slung a beach towel over her shoulder and led Alli out into the backyard. "I think he'll remember this time."

Alli brightened. "I hope so. I want to tell him about all this."

"You know, your dad loves you very much." Jolie unlatched the gate and she and Alli walked onto the concrete surrounding the pool.

"I know he does," Alli said, hanging back slightly as all the girls stopped playing and turned their attention to her.

"Hi, Aunt Jolie," a few of the girls chorused.

"Hi," Jolie answered. "This is my friend Alli. She's my guest. Who can show her a good time?"

"I can!" Suzy shouted. She swam over to the edge closest

to Jolie's feet. Although nowhere near Alli's age, Suzy liked to be in the thick of things.

Another girl approached, her long hair floating atop the water. "How old are you?" she asked Alli.

"Ten. Eleven in September," Alli answered.

"That means you're my age. I'm Rebecca. Not Becky or Becca but Rebecca."

"Alli," Alli said.

"Jump in," Rebecca commanded.

"Who's on guard duty?" Jolie asked.

"I am." One of the teenagers raised her hand. She was related somehow, like a second cousin once removed or something. "I'm actually certified. Your mom's paying me to work this weekend. I need the money for college."

"Then I'll leave Alli with you."

Alli hadn't gotten in the water yet and she looked a bit scared. "You coming?" Rebecca asked. A few of the other girls had arrived and were watching Alli. Jolie could see why Alli might feel intimated.

"I'll watch you swim for a few minutes," Jolie told Alli. "Go on. I bet the water temperature's perfect. My dad heats the pool if it's the least bit too cold." She placed Alli's towel on a nearby table. Jolie removed her sandals and sat on the edge of the pool so she could dangle her legs in. The water was just right.

Alli used the stairs to enter the pool. She waded in slowly, the girls circling her and clamoring for her attention. Then she braved the shock and immersed herself fully, resurfacing to fling water out of her hair. Soon she was off playing with the rest of the girls, her nervousness gone.

"Mom said you'd arrived," Jennifer said to Jolie about ten minutes later. The gate clicked as it closed behind her.

"Yeah, we got here a little while ago. I'm just making

sure Alli's going to be okay," Jolie replied as she watched the kids swim. So far Jolie had been unable to make herself leave the pool area.

Jennifer observed the scene for a moment. "She's fine."

"I know."

"Then why haven't you come back up to the house? Megan's certified and on duty."

"Alli's been showing me some of her tricks." As if on cue, Alli did a handstand in the shallow end. "She's a regular fish. She's been down the slide a few times and off the diving board."

"So let her play and get to know everyone," Jennifer said.

Jolie kept her gaze on Alli, waiting until she resurfaced. Alli saw Jolie and waved. "I'll be there in a while. Go on. I don't want to keep you," Jolie said.

Jennifer didn't move. "Jolie. She'll be fine. She's a kid."

Jolie turned to look at her sister then. "But what if she isn't? What if something happens? What if she needs me?"

Jennifer stood and reached for Jolie's hand. "I know how hard this weekend is for you, but she'll be fine. Ethan, that's his name, right? He's already playing Wiffleball."

"Ethan's tougher," Jolie said, responding to her sister's insistent tug and rising to her feet. But Jen was right. She had to shake off the anxiety. Alli wasn't Ruthie. Alli was a healthy ten-year-old, not a fragile baby.

"Alli, I'm going up to the house," Jolie called. "Are you fine here by yourself?"

Alli glanced at the house, which was a mere fifty feet away. She nodded. "I'm good."

"We'll take care of her, Aunt Jolie," Rebecca said, and both girls dove back beneath the water.

"So whose daughter is she?" Jennifer asked as they left the pool area.

Jolie knew what her sister meant. "I tutored Ethan and Alli after school. Their dad is away unexpectedly and asked for my help. We're friends."

"So is he divorced?" Jen asked, waving to someone.

Jolie shook her head. "Widowed. Their mother died five years ago."

The two women fell into step. "And you met him when he came to school and…"

"I related to the kids. Like I said, Hank and I are friends. Nothing more. It'd be unprofessional."

"You aren't their teacher anymore, and this seems like a big favor to ask of someone who's just a friend," Jen stated.

Darn her sister's logic. "I'm just babysitting. You know me. I took care of all the strays that wandered onto the farm. The family needed help. I'd do it even if Hank was married."

"Uh-huh." Jennifer didn't seem very convinced.

"You can meet him tomorrow when he picks up the kids."

"He's coming here?" Jennifer squeaked.

"Yeah, why not?"

"You are brave." Jennifer gave an incredulous shake of her head.

"I'm not worried about him meeting everyone. I don't think he's going to be staying, anyway, but if he does, he'll just be one more person hanging around."

"You amaze me," Jennifer said. "I think you've fallen for him."

Jolie scoffed. "That's ludicrous. If anything, I've fallen for his kids."

Ethan and Alli were adorable and extremely personable.

When she was with them she could pretend they were hers. Her child, had she lived, would have been about their age.

"I know what you're thinking," Jennifer said.

"No, trust me, you don't," Jolie replied defensively. "It's hard. You'd think after all this time the memory would go away."

Her sister's eyes shone with sympathy. "Her death wasn't your fault."

Jolie emitted a guttural noise that was half cry, half bitter laugh. "I know, but try telling my heart that. Deep down I'll always wonder if there was something I could have done."

Jennifer wrapped her arms around Jolie's shoulders. "No one blames you."

"Reggie did."

"Reggie's a jerk." They'd reached the deck and screened-in porch. "Let's go socialize with all these people we only see once a year. Let's hope Great-aunt Edna doesn't lose her dentures in the salad this time."

Jolie stuck out her tongue. "Eww. That was gross."

"You weren't the one who had to fish them out!"

As both sisters laughed and Jolie's mood lightened, she realized that she had to focus on the present, the here and now.

As always with Tomlinson parties, the day went by far too fast, a blur of activity. Jolie checked on the twins often—both of them were having a great time with their new friends.

When Hank called around nine, Alli was nearby so Jolie handed her the phone.

"Hi, Daddy," Alli said, her fingers clutching Jolie's cell phone. "Yes, I'm having a great time. I went swimming and saw a foal." She listened. "Uh-huh. I made new friends. Lots." She glanced shyly at Jolie. "She's taking good care of us."

The corners of Jolie's mouth lifted and she moved a few feet away to give Alli more privacy. They were on the screened porch, and outside a group of kids, including Ethan, were trying to catch lightning bugs.

"Ethan. Your dad's on the phone."

"Tell him I'll talk to him tomorrow," he shouted as he raced after an escaping yellow flicker.

Alli padded over and handed Jolie the phone. "I'm done."

"You can go out there, too," Jolie told her.

"Go where?" Hank asked, realizing he had Jolie on the end of the line.

"The kids are chasing lightning bugs," Jolie replied. "Ethan said he'd talk to you tomorrow."

"Oh." Hank sounded disappointed. "He does that sometimes when I'm gone a lot. He's not a conversationalist."

"Some children aren't." Jolie tracked Alli's movements, locating her near a bunch of bushes.

"Have I said thank-you enough?" Hank asked. "Alli told me they're having a wonderful time."

"You have great children." Ethan had found a jar and he was helping his sister put a bug inside. Later all the insects would be freed, unharmed.

"You're great with them. I'm in debt to you."

"Really, it's nothing. Stop being a broken record."

"It *is* something, so stop protesting. I haven't changed my mind."

"About what?"

"About you. You're not their teacher anymore."

Her heart raced. "No, I'm not."

"So there's no reason for you to say no when I ask you out again."

"Uh—"

"Have a good night and I'll see you tomorrow," Hank

said, disconnecting before she could object. She stared at her phone, but it remained silent.

The kids played for a while longer, and around ten everyone headed off to bed. Jolie checked on Ethan; he'd stretched out on a cot sandwiched between Avery's and Skip's. She told Ethan good-night, knowing he was safe, since her brother Bill would do sleep-in-the-barn duty.

Alli was next, and Jolie adjusted her sleeping bag. A ceiling fan circled on the porch. The late-May day had been in the low nineties with no humidity, and the night would be a comfortable seventy-five.

"Good night, Alli. I'll be right through that doorway if you need me or if you have any bad dreams."

Alli had brought Veronica, her doll, and she snuggled it close. A few of the other children had already drifted off to sleep, but some of the older girls were still giggling. Jennifer stood in the hall doorway, her "Shh" designed to end any nonsense and get even the older girls to sleep quickly.

"Jolie?" Alli whispered, and Jolie leaned over. "No, closer," Alli implored, so Jolie squatted down next to her.

"What is it?"

Alli propped her head on her elbow and brought her face closer. Jolie didn't realize what the little girl was planning until the moment her lips lightly brushed Jolie's cheek. "Good night, Jolie. I love you."

"I love you, too," Jolie answered, her reply honest and raw. While Alli's words were like a vise on her heart, she wouldn't let them go unanswered lest Alli feel unloved.

"You'd make a good mommy," Alli said, and then she turned her face to the side, snuggled deeper into the blanket and closed her eyes.

Jolie straightened, her gaze catching her sister's. Jolie could feel the tears gathering in her eyes, so she did what any mature woman would do when confronted with emotions she didn't want to deal with. She fled into her bedroom and closed the door.

"SO WHERE ARE your kids again?" Peter asked as Hank returned to the table. There were a few people lingering after the late dinner.

"They're spending the night at Jolie's parents' farm," Hank told his boss and mentor.

"And Jolie is...?" Peter prodded.

"She was their teacher. Well, Ethan's technically. But she tutored both of them."

Peter leaned back slightly. "I sense there's more to it than that."

"I like her," Hank admitted.

Peter arched his eyebrow.

"A lot," Hank confessed. "She's the first woman who has caught my attention in a long time. I'm determined to take her out on a real date, but so far she's put me off. She thought it would be inappropriate since she was Ethan's teacher."

"And now school's out."

"Exactly," Hank said, reaching for his coffee cup. "I haven't felt a flicker of real interest in...forever, and I'd like to take her out a few times. See where things lead."

"Well, you know I wholeheartedly support that," Peter said. "Do you think you can convince her to say yes?"

Hank thought of Jolie. She made his heart race, made him feel things he hadn't felt since Amanda. "I'm certainly going to try."

Chapter Eight

The sun was already high in the midday sky when Hank reached the gravel driveway of the Tomlinson farm. The property was northwest of Branson and didn't border the lake. Instead, it consisted of groves of trees, fields of corn and wide-open pastures containing grazing cattle. While the farm was only a half-hour drive from Branson, the city seemed like a distant memory.

So Jolie had grown up here, Hank mused as he continued down the mile-long, oak tree-lined drive. His car rattled over a metal bridge. Below were the remains of the original, low-water concrete bridge that had served until this one was built.

The driveway curved to the right and he could see a white farmhouse up on a slight hill. The view had the aura of a Norman Rockwell painting, if you didn't count the plethora of parked cars, tents, campers, an inflatable bounce house and the crowd of people.

He parked his Lexus and strolled up the driveway toward the house. He could hear joyous shrieks from inside the bounce house, but couldn't tell if any of the voices belonged to his children. He scanned the field where a group played Wiffleball, then turned his attention to the group of men playing washers. His nose inhaled the pungent smell of barbecue and his stomach grumbled. It was a little after one and he'd skipped lunch.

He passed a few people, nodded hellos to some kids who raced by, and headed toward the back of the house, where it appeared even more of Jolie's family were congregated. There had to be more than a hundred people here.

"Hi," an older woman said as he rounded the corner and stepped into the backyard. Here an assortment of picnic tables had been covered with red-and-white plastic tablecloths. At many, families ate corn on the cob, coleslaw, hamburgers, hot dogs and short ribs. Hank's stomach rumbled again.

"Hi. I'm Hank. Can you tell me where Jolie is?" he asked the woman.

She blinked. "Let me think. I'm not sure where I saw her last, maybe doing some lunch cleanup, but that's her sister Jennifer right over there. Maudie should also be nearby."

The woman pointed and Hank saw three women standing together. One had features similar to Jolie's. "So that's her sister in the red shirt?" Hank clarified. He had no idea who Maudie was.

"Yes."

"Thanks." He approached Jennifer, who was covering some of the serving dishes with plastic wrap.

"Hi. Are you Jennifer? I'm looking for Jolie. Can you tell me where she is?"

She faced him, and he saw that her eyes were blue, not green, and her hair was darker than Jolie's. "You must be Hank. We've all been expecting you," Jennifer said.

"Mom, Hank's here," she shouted. Hank's stomach flipped. He wasn't dating Jolie, but his children had spent the night at the farm. And now it looked as if he was about to meet her family.

Jolie's mother stood about ten feet away. She wiped her hands on her striped apron and approached. "I'm Maudie. Your children have been absolute delights and no trouble at all." She smiled warmly at Hank and he felt his tension ease. "They're on a trail ride. They left about ten minutes ago."

"Oh."

Disappointment at not being able to hug his kids must have shown on his face, for Maudie said, "Now don't worry. Jolie's with them and she's a pro. Our horses are very docile. They'll be back in a little bit."

He glanced at his watch. He'd intended to pick up the children and leave quickly to give Jolie her free time back.

"Have you eaten?" Maudie asked.

He shook his head.

"Well, we have plenty, so get yourself a plate. We'll be serving food all day. We've got a pig roasting on the spit if you decide to stay for dinner. I know your kids want to."

"Uh…" Hank didn't quite know how to respond to her invitation, so he grabbed one of the paper plates and began filling it with food.

He sat at a table and had almost finished eating when a thirtysomething male plopped down on the bench across from him. "So you're Hank."

"I am," Hank said.

"I'm Lance. Jolie's twin."

"Nice to meet you," Hank said. He gestured with his fork. "This blueberry cobbler's delicious."

"It's my mom's recipe," Lance said. He had a glass of iced tea in his hand and he took a drink before asking, "So what's going on between you and my sister?"

Hank had no idea. "She tells me we're friends."

"And that's it?" Lance didn't seem too happy with that answer.

"As far as I know," Hank replied, digging into a piece of chocolate cake next. He was a sucker for desserts. "Ethan was a student in her class. She volunteered to help me out."

Lance tilted his head. "That's pretty much what she told us." He shrugged and gazed past Hank as if sending a message.

Hank turned around to see Maudie and Jennifer watching. They immediately scattered. "What's going on?"

"Nothing. Jolie doesn't date much. Her ex was a jerk and none of us liked the last guy she dated. We just wanted to know your intentions."

Even though he planned on asking Jolie out he wasn't going to share that piece of information with Lance.

"It's not up to me. She's the one calling the shots."

"So you like her," Lance pressed.

"We're friends," Hank repeated. A group of horseback riders rode into the clearing, capturing the men's attention.

"That'll be them," Lance said. "Come on, I'll take you down to the barn."

Hank followed Lance. His dress shoes were covered in dust by the time they stepped up to the corral fence. Jolie led the ten-horse line, and Hank swallowed as she dismounted and opened the gate so everyone could enter.

"Lance, do me a favor and close this gate," Jolie called as she led her horse inside.

"Hi, Daddy!" Alli waved from the back of a palomino before again grabbing the saddle horn. Hank returned his daughter's greeting and watched as Jolie reached for Alli's reins and led the horse to a place along the fence.

Ethan, near the end of the line, waved, too, but not as vigorously as Alli. Lance shut the gate behind the last rider, and soon Alli climbed through the fence rails and reached her dad's side. "Did you see me?"

"I did," Hank said as he gave her a hug. He tapped the cowboy hat on her head. "Did Jolie lend you this?"

"Yep. Her mom even had some boots I could wear." She held out her foot and pointed a toe. "The jeans and shirt are mine."

"I thought I recognized those." Hank laughed. Ethan approached, but as if aware of the other guys, didn't step close enough for a hug. "Nice ride?" Hank asked.

"Yeah," Ethan replied. He glanced over his shoulder. "Do we have to leave right now? A few of the guys and I are going down to the pond to fish."

Hank knew when to change his mind, especially after seeing the two hopeful expressions in front of him. "I guess we can stay a while longer. I want to talk to Jolie, anyway."

"Cool. Hey, I can stay!" Ethan called to his friends. "Thanks, Dad. See you later." Before Hank could give Ethan a return time, the boys had taken off.

"I hope he wasn't supposed to help with the horses," Hank told Alli.

Jolie overheard them and approached. "It's fine. My sister's going to take another group of kids out in a few minutes. After that we'll unsaddle the horses and turn them out to pasture for the rest of the day."

"Okay," Hank said. "I just don't want him to shirk his responsibilities."

"Don't worry," Jolie said. She grinned. "Any trouble finding the place?"

"No, it was easy. Great directions. Thanks."

Hank waited, marveling at the sudden awkwardness of the moment. He couldn't help staring at Jolie, who looked amazing in her casual clothes. She wore a spaghetti-strap tank top, a pair of jeans that fit like gloves, and riding boots. Her hair was in a ponytail, but instead of a cowboy hat, she'd pulled everything through the back of a Kansas City Royals ball cap. She was a goddess with a face as fresh as an angel's.

"So since you're staying, shall we go back up to the house? Unless you'd like to check on the foal," Jolie told Alli.

"Your mom said we shouldn't bother him so much," Alli said.

"One last peek won't hurt," Jolie replied.

In the barn Hank lifted his daughter so she could look down into the stall. The mare blinked at them once. The foal, a colt, was on his feet behind his mother, and he peered around, his full white face visible.

"He's a paint horse," Alli told her dad as he set her back on the ground.

"How many horses do you have?" Hank asked as they made their way back up to the house.

"About fifteen," Jolie replied. "Dad boards a few for friends."

Hank was confused. "So this is a working farm. I thought your dad was a school superintendent."

"Was. He retired a while ago. My dad and my brother Bill manage the place. Have you met them yet?"

Jolie's gait easily matched his, so Hank scooped up Alli, whose legs were shorter than theirs, and gave her a piggyback ride. "I met your mom, Lance and Jennifer."

"Hopefully that wasn't too bad. They can be…" Jolie paused.

"Nosy? Protective?"

"All of the above?" Jolie said.

"They made up for it by feeding me some good grub," Hank replied.

"Grub?" Alli asked.

Hank smiled. "A country expression. Grub means food."

"Oh. Okay." He put his daughter down and she looked around until she spotted her friends. "Can…may I go play with the girls?"

"Go ahead," Hank said, and Alli raced off. He faced Jolie. "I guess it's just you and me. Well, and all these other people."

Jolie laughed. "If you want, I'll introduce you around. There might be a quiz at the end, but don't worry, I may miss a few names, too. This reunion keeps getting bigger and bigger. I meet someone new every year."

Hank followed her to a seating area inside a small gazebo. She gestured to an Adirondack chair and sat in the one across from it. "How late will you stay?" she asked.

He shrugged. "I don't know."

"I should warn you—there are fireworks tonight. Dad hires a company to do a small show. The twins know about it and they've been scheming all day to get you say yes."

"They do love fireworks," Hank admitted. "We don't have to leave. I just don't want to be a bother. Your brother already asked what was going on between us."

"I told them we were friends."

"Which is what I said since that's what you told me last night. He seemed a bit…"

"Probably disappointed." Jolie brushed off the rest of Hank's statement before he could finish. "My family evaluates everyone as a potential marriage mate. Ignore them. They mean well, but they're rather misguided. I'm the only single one in the group."

"You like being single?" Hank asked. Maybe that was the reason she'd said no.

She shrugged. "I'm used to it. It's not necessarily a bad thing. I'm pretty set in my ways, so I can be rather high maintenance and I admit it."

"I dated a few times about a year after my wife died. No

one interested me, but even if they had, my priority was being home with the kids. Plus, my job isn't exactly nine to five."

She chuckled. "I've noticed."

He laughed, too. "Yeah, I guess you would have. However, I'm hoping to change."

"Has it always been like this?"

He nodded. "Pretty much. In the beginning it was a lot of fun. Premier is a family-oriented chain. So Amanda and I always had functions to attend. At last night's dinner, I was the only one without a spouse."

"Is that bad?"

"My bosses are all happily married, and they prefer even numbers. Even after the children were born, Amanda attended tons of social events."

Jolie placed a hand on his arm and he liked her touch. "It must have been hard to lose her."

"Devastating. It's like there's a big hole that I can't fill. For years I ignored it."

"That's easiest," Jolie said.

Her insight was spot-on. "Exactly. I immersed myself in work, which is something I'm good at. I'm trying to parent my kids, which is something I'm not so good at."

"But you are," Jolie insisted. "You're better than plenty of parents I've seen. Some don't care at all. Others have children for all the wrong reasons, such as trying to get someone to love them. I've seen parents who hate each other so much that their children become pawns in the battle. You love those kids and they know it. Just look at how Alli hugged you the moment she saw you."

That had felt wonderful. "You make it sound so simple," he said. "You know exactly what to say."

Jolie averted her eyes. "I'm just being a good friend."

"Which I haven't reciprocated. It's been all one-sided—you give, I take." He felt angry with himself when he realized how much he'd taken advantage of her kindness. "I've used you. I'm sorry. I guess I was unprepared for how much help I'd need when I moved here. My job has always been demanding. Once Amanda and I had the kids, she stayed home and I worked. She understood the long hours, for I'd always had them. I guess she knew what she was getting into when she married me. She used to joke, 'Hi, my name's Amanda and I married a workaholic.'"

His gaze clouded a little. "Hindsight's twenty-twenty and now I realize she wanted me home more with the twins. But I was busy building my career and her mother was always there and I felt like a third wheel. As babies, Ethan and Alli were tiny. I thought I might break them or something. It's silly, but they seemed so fragile. Work was an excuse to stay away and let Amanda do the mothering thing."

"I can understand your fear that you would somehow harm them," she said. Her hand was still on his arm and she patted him lightly. He had the sudden urge to pull her to him and kiss her.

They were friends, but Hank wanted more. He wanted to feel again, to know he wasn't emotionally dead. Last night he'd determined to set a first date. But today he realized he didn't want to use Jolie just as a way to get back out there. He really liked her and wanted to get to know her.

He wanted a relationship, not a date.

A group of girls shrieked with laughter as they rounded the corner and then disappeared from sight. He took Jolie's hand from his arm and lifted it to his lips. He briefly kissed her soft skin before letting go. "Thank you for listening, but I don't want to use you as a sounding board. You've already done so much."

He sighed and told her what troubled him now. "Ethan and Alli have had more fun this weekend with you than I've probably given them all their lives."

JOLIE STARED at Hank. She was one of those people who believed that God put people in your life for certain reasons. With Hank, she'd assumed her role was to help him and the children through this transition to Missouri and life on their own, nothing more. "Don't say that," she said. "You are a great father. Those kids love you."

"I'm not doubting that. Okay, maybe I am a little," he admitted. "But I have to stand on my own two feet. I can't do what I did with Amanda's mother. I depended on Sylvia. She made my life easier. I refuse to do the same with you. I like you. I want to date you, not delegate to you."

His honesty impressed her. Few men in her past had ever been so open. But Hank wasn't most men. There was depth to him. He was driven. He wasn't the kind of guy who could settle for second best. She'd had many students like Hank over the years. That type A personality took them to the top, but even then they craved more. Something was always missing.

"It's okay to be flawed," she said. "I'm certainly not perfect. I've failed more times than I can count."

"I'm the one who let people down," Hank said.

Jolie stared at him. "You think I haven't done that?"

He shook his head. "You're wonderful. I see how you interact with my children and with the others in your class. It impresses me how much you care."

"You care, too," she protested.

"But it's not enough," he said. "No matter what I do, it's never enough. I can't expect anyone to understand how that feels—the helplessness of losing someone."

"The powerlessness," Jolie said.

His eyes widened. "You can't have been there."

"Someone I loved very much died and I couldn't do anything about it," she told him. The pain in her chest sharpened.

"I've been insensitive. I forgot you were married."

"I wasn't talking about my ex-husband," Jolie said. She inhaled a deep breath. "I was talking about my daughter. She was in my care, and she died."

Chapter Nine

Hank looked stunned, and Jolie couldn't believe she'd shared her tragic past with him. It wasn't something she ever did with newer acquaintances.

Maybe she'd wanted to assuage his guilt. Maybe she'd wanted to take herself off the pedestal on which he'd mistakenly placed her. Maybe she'd needed to say the words as a way not to forget that it had been this weekend, exactly nine years ago, that her world had fallen apart.

"I'm sorry," Hank said, his tone uneasy as he apparently digested the situation and tried to figure out how best to handle it. "I didn't know. I—"

"Don't feel bad," Jolie said, trying to make her voice light. "I just wanted to let you know that you're not alone, that you're not the only one who has gone through a tragedy like this. I understand what you've been through…what you're still enduring. The hurt, the anguish, the what-if, the why-me questions. The damning of fate. Even worse is everyone's well-meaning sympathy, which only makes the pain sharper."

"You've nailed it," Hank said.

"So don't have any illusions about me," Jolie said. "I'm not as wonderful as you think. As a mom, I failed."

"Do you mind telling me what happened?"

"SIDS," Jolie replied. She drew a deep breath and tried not to cry. "Everyone said it wasn't my fault, but I couldn't accept that. I envy you. You had time to say goodbye. My daughter was just gone. That's my deepest regret."

They sat there without speaking for almost five minutes. Words weren't necessary as, lost in their own thoughts, they watched the world around them. Children played. The wind carried shrieks and laughter and the occasional clang of horseshoes. Somewhere a horse whinnied and a dog barked. A rooster crowed, despite it being three o'clock in the afternoon.

"Thank you," Hank said, breaking the silence. He placed his right hand on her left, the pressure warm and welcome.

"I'm not sure I did anything," Jolie said, enjoying his touch.

"No, you did. Just by sharing. It hammered home that I'm not the only one who's lost something precious."

"It's easy to get tunnel vision. Reggie blamed me for Ruthie's death, and I blamed myself, as well. It didn't take long for our marriage to fall apart—not that we didn't have problems beforehand. It took me a long time to move past what happened."

"I think my biggest worry is that the kids won't remember her," Hank admitted.

"They always will. Amanda gave them life."

They fell silent again as a small group of young children came racing through the yard, chasing a boy who held several kites in his hand. Jolie automatically tilted her head to assess the situation, and relaxed when she heard the shrieks of laughter. All was okay and within a few minutes, the kids were in a wide-open space and letting the kites fly.

"I'm glad I'm here," Hank said, turning his attention away from the scene.

"You're welcome to stay. The more the merrier, my parents always say. Ethan and Alli are having a great time."

"No, I meant I'm glad I'm here, with *you,*" Hank clarified. "I'm not giving up. If anything, I'm even more convinced that I want you to say yes."

His hand was still on hers. "I..." she began.

"I feel a connection with you," Hank continued as she faltered. "Part of me really wants to explore this. The other part admits to being nervous as hell. But I can't get you out of my mind."

"I'm not so special, just a regular woman," she protested. He was so different from her ex and from Chad, who'd never paid her this many compliments.

"Don't sell yourself short. You're a beautiful and intelligent woman. We have fun together and I enjoy our talks. I'd really like to get to know you better. But if you tell me my attentions are unwelcome, I won't bother you anymore."

"They are welcome."

He visibly relaxed. "Good."

"But I still have to say no. We just met. It's too soon."

"No, it's not. I've waited five years and realized one thing. Life's too short not to be living it to the fullest. I don't want to miss out on something great because of some mysterious relationship rules I'm supposed to follow. I've been out of the dating market for so long I don't even know what the rules are. What I do know is that I feel something for you that I'd like to explore. So live a little. If I asked you out again, would you say yes?" The mood had lightened considerably.

"Are you ever going to give up?" Jolie arched a brow, studying him.

"No."

"Well, I'm no longer your children's teacher, so I guess

there's no ethical dilemma," Jolie said. "Yes, Hank. I'd love to go out with you."

"Finally!" Hank chuckled, lifting her hand to his lips and giving it a light kiss. Her skin tingled. "How about next weekend? If that goes well, then how about the weekend after that?"

Jolie winced. "Next weekend sounds fine. The one after that? Not unless you want to accompany me to my cousin's wedding. The event means a lot to my mother. However, the reception is at the Nolter, so that might be awkward for you."

"Yes, I'll go," Hank said easily.

Jolie blinked. "Really? You don't mind spending most of the day with my family?" she asked, marveling that they were talking about a second date long before even going on the first.

"I think it'll be fine and fun. I like your family," Hank said.

"I think they like you, too," Jolie admitted.

"That's good, because they're standing over there keeping an eye on us. I'll try to resist the urge to kiss you, since they're watching."

"That'll spare me the questioning," Jolie said, nevertheless feeling a little bereft. Darn, she wanted that kiss!

"Later," Hank promised as if reading her mind. He released her hand when Ethan came running up, Alli right behind him.

"Hey, Dad! There you are! Are we staying? Everyone's going down to the creek and I want to go," Ethan said, not even winded as he climbed the gazebo stairs. Alli hesitated at the bottom.

"We'll stay until after the fireworks," Hank announced.

"Yay!" Alli shouted. She ran off, this time with Ethan at *her* heels.

Jolie used the kids' departure as an opportunity to stand. "We should probably make sure there's an adult supervising at the creek. There should be, but it'll get us out from under my mother's watchful eye."

"Good idea." Hank rose and followed her.

BY THE END of the evening, Hank had met no fewer than six dozen people. Everyone had been warm and welcoming, but it was the woman sitting beside him on the blanket that interested him most.

He'd been floored by Jolie's revelation that she'd lost her baby to SIDS. He'd instantly wanted to take her in his arms and comfort her.

Jolie had been right when she'd said that memories became fuzzy. While he'd never forget Amanda, certain details from their relationship had faded. In the first year following her death, anyone wearing her favorite perfume had made him melancholy. Now he couldn't identify the scent. He could easily picture her smile, but not necessarily her favorite sweater, except that she'd had it for years and it was some shade of gray.

At first he'd clung to the memories, rehashing them in his mind so he wouldn't forget. He'd gone through the photo albums, watched the videos so he'd remember the huskiness of her voice or the way her blond hair flew up in the wind. He'd clung to those things, not recognizing that, as part of time's healing powers, those memories needed to become hazy.

If he was to love again and not spend the next fifty-odd years alone, he'd have to let her go and move on. She'd always be with him in his heart, though. Some of Amanda's last words to him had been that she wanted him to love again. She hadn't wanted him to be by himself for the rest of his life. He'd scoffed at her deathbed request. He'd been too emotional to see his wife's wisdom.

She hadn't meant immediately, but when he was ready. That time had come.

"Are you okay?" Jolie glanced over at him. Both Ethan and Alli, who sat in front of them, swiveled their heads.

"Yeah," Hank said, resisting the urge to touch Jolie's hand as an orange starburst lit the night sky. As the fireworks went on, Hank wanted nothing more than to cover Jolie's hand with his as he'd done earlier today. But his children might see, and Jolie had suggested talking to them first, explaining the change in their relationship before the children saw any physical evidence, like hand-holding.

The crowd gave the requisite oohs and ahhs to the display. The day had been good, Hank decided. Good food. Good company. Good karma. He'd chosen correctly when he'd decided to move to Branson. Otherwise, he'd never have met Jolie. Alli snuggled back against him, and he drew his daughter into the crook of his arm.

This was what Amanda would want. She'd want her family to be together, happy and whole. She'd want them moving forward, embracing life again. For the first time in five years, a sense of contentment settled over Hank.

"SO YOU'RE SURE you're okay to drive? You know you can stay here," Jolie said. She stood by Hank's car twenty minutes after the fireworks had ended. The children were in the house grabbing their things. It was past ten, and Hank was ready to take Ethan and Alli home.

"Yeah. I'm not tired and I only had one beer with dinner, hours ago."

"I didn't mean that. You just seemed a little emotional during the fireworks."

"Amanda always loved fireworks," Hank replied. He reached forward and pulled Jolie to him. "I think I said goodbye to her tonight."

"You never truly say goodbye," Jolie said.

"No, but you let go. You grab what's in front of you and not what's behind. She wanted me to move on. She told me that, but I couldn't even fathom what she meant. Until tonight."

"Wow." Jolie snuggled closer, enjoying the warmth of being pressed against his chest.

"You even fit me."

"I'm so tall," Jolie said.

"Which is perfect. Your mouth, it's right here in front of mine. I almost kissed you that night at the hotel. I can't tell you how tempted I was, how tempted I still am."

"I wanted you to kiss me," she admitted, her voice a little breathless in anticipation. He held her tight.

With a sort of groan of defeat, he angled his head and brought his mouth to hers. His touch was light and gentle, almost tentative. "I haven't done this in a while," he whispered.

"You're doing fine so far," she replied, pressing her lips to his for a quick kiss before saying, "See?"

"Uh-huh," Hank said, dipping to connect with her again. His mouth was more insistent in its exploration of hers this time, nibbling her lips as he learned the feel of her. She let him support her weight as his hands moved to cup her face and his fingers threaded into her hair.

"Wow," Jolie said as she drew back, hearing movement on the pavement behind her.

Hank kept his forehead bent toward hers and then reluctantly let her go as Ethan said, "Hey, Dad, whatcha doing with Ms. Tomlinson?"

"Jolie," Alli corrected her brother before addressing

her dad. "Why are you kissing her, Dad? Is she going to be our new mom?"

"No such thing as privacy," Hank whispered so only Jolie heard. Then he released her and turned to his children. "Jolie and I are kissing and we're talking about dating."

"So is she going to be our new mom?" Alli repeated.

"That's not exactly how it works," Jolie said. "Your dad and I just met. People don't just meet and get married."

"I got married to Bobby Jones on the playground during recess."

"She even kissed him!" Ethan said.

Hank's eyebrows shot up and Jolie gave him a confused shrug. "I'm not on playground duty during lunch and I hadn't heard about this," she told him.

"It was the last week of school. He married Becky the next day," Alli said, apparently not too concerned about Bobby's bigamy.

"Well, when you're bigger you get married to one person and for a lot longer," Jolie said.

"Till death do you part," Alli parroted.

"So you kissed a boy?" Hank asked.

"It was just on the cheek. It was nothing." Alli shrugged. "The girls dared me to do it."

"She didn't back down, either," Ethan said.

"Obviously we need a better recess monitor," Jolie told Hank. She picked up Alli's suitcase. "Let's get this in the car so you and your dad can get going."

Shortly, they had everything loaded and Hank started the engine. Ethan and Alli climbed into the backseat. Even though the lights were off inside the car, Hank and Jolie were very aware of their rapt audience.

"I hadn't planned on explaining dating to them this soon," Hank said. "We'll talk on the way home."

"That may be for the best," Jolie said. "Kids are smart. They pick up on things you'd never imagine."

"How about I call you tomorrow?" Hank asked. "Will you be busy?"

"I'll spend most of the weekend out here helping my parents. Then I have a week off before teaching summer school."

"Would Friday night work for our date? Maybe a show on the strip? I have a concierge who can procure tickets to anything."

"Even though I've lived here all my life, I haven't seen many shows. You do know how to tempt someone, don't you?"

"I hope so," Hank said with a grin. "Think about Friday and let me know what you'd like to do. I'll phone you Tuesday. That way you'll have some uninterrupted time with your folks."

She nodded and he leaned toward her and dropped a light kiss on her lips. "Until then."

Jolie stood in the yard, watching until Hank's taillights disappeared from view. Then she turned and strolled back toward the house.

"SO DID HANK have a nice time?" Maudie asked when Jolie entered the kitchen. Jolie blinked as her eyes adjusted to the bright light. It was now a little after eleven, and the farm was settling down to sleep. Tomorrow was Sunday, and her father always arranged for church services to be held outside at 10:00 a.m. The boys had finished setting up folding chairs on the lawn and, in the kitchen, her mother, Jennifer and a few aunts and cousins were cleaning up from dinner and preparing Sunday's brunch.

"He and his kids had a lovely time. They had nothing but

compliments. Thank you so much for letting them come," Jolie said.

"Everyone's welcome. We especially enjoyed meeting him. He seems like a very nice man." Her mother dried the outside and inside of a stew pot and passed it to Jen so she could put it away.

Jolie leaned her hip against the counter. "What, no twenty questions?" She glanced at her sister, who kept her head oddly averted. "Okay, what is going on? You both grill me about every man I even mention. So nothing on Hank? A guy who kissed me outside?"

"Did he? We hadn't noticed," Maudie said, her blush giving her away.

"Don't listen to her, Jolie. Mom was at the window as if she was watching a movie," Jen said, unable to resist.

"I'd already pegged her for a liar," Jolie said.

Her mom rolled her eyes heavenward and gave a sheepish grin. "Please, not a liar. I was just trying to give you space. Treat you like an adult."

"Which is why you were watching me?" Jolie asked good-naturedly. She grabbed the rag Jen tossed and reached for the pot lid her mother had just finished washing. "Somehow this family knows everyone's business the moment it happens."

"Listening at doors and looking out windows is an art form," Jen inserted.

"True, so don't go all 'you need your space' on my behalf. I know you're dying for the details," Jolie said.

"Which are?" Jen prodded.

"He asked me out for Friday night and I said yes. I also asked him to go to the wedding, and assuming all goes well on Friday, he agreed. End of story."

"You have a date to the wedding? A man?" Maudie

paused, fingers in the dish soap. She seemed shocked and Jen snickered.

"So much for listening," Jen said.

"I believe I just said I have a date," Jolie replied now that she had her mom's full attention. "Hank agreed to go."

"Oh, thank heaven," Maudie said and Jolie resisted the urge to swat her with the dishrag.

"I can get dates with men," Jolie objected.

"You don't have a good track record," her mother said. "And as much as I love all your girlfriends, there's no way I can go to this shindig and have my sister lord it over me that you can't find a man."

"I don't know why you give Aunt Renee so much credence, anyway," Jolie said. "Jen and I don't."

"Renee's just a different type," Maudie said. "If she hadn't been born after me and I hadn't seen her in the hospital myself, I'd swear my mother brought home the wrong child. You notice she only came for a little while today. We've never been that close. That's why I treasure the fact that this family is so tight. I have what money can't buy."

"Now don't go all sentimental on us," Jen said, pleased. "Jolie's got a date. That's not a reason to turn weepy. Heck, we should shoot off some more fireworks."

"We'll save those until she's married," Maudie joked, momentary melancholy passing.

"That'll take forever," Lance said, entering the kitchen. Jolie tossed the dish towel, but he caught it before it hit him in the chest. "What's that for?"

"Because you're a jerk," Jolie said. "You don't even know what's going on."

"True, but I do know that you and marriage don't mix," Lance teased.

"Jolie has a date," Jen told her brother.

"'Bout time," Lance said, snagging a plate and loading it up with some leftovers. "I'm headed down to the barn. Bill had last night's shift, so I said I'd take today."

"Well, we'll see you in the morning," Maudie told Lance, giving him a quick kiss on the cheek before he left, plate in hand.

"I'm going to turn in, too," Jolie said. "Oh, Mom, one last thing. Alli would like to take piano lessons. Her mother used to play and Alli's got a baby grand sitting in the suite."

"I'd be happy to teach her. Let's talk about it tomorrow. I'll look at my schedule and you can let Hank know the times I have available."

"Sounds good." Jolie gave hugs to her sister and mother and headed upstairs to bed.

As she entered her bedroom her cell phone buzzed once. Worried about waking the girls sleeping on the sunporch, Jolie grabbed the phone quickly. "Hello?"

"Did I wake you?" Hank's voice rumbled through the line and Jolie's heart jumped.

"No, I was just getting ready for bed," she said. "Are Ethan and Alli asleep?"

"They couldn't keep their eyes open in the car. That's why I'm calling. I wanted to thank you again. We had a wonderful time this weekend—me and the kids."

"It was nothing," she said, flattered by his attention.

"You're wrong, but I won't argue with you about that now. Go to bed and get some much-needed rest. I'll talk to you later this week."

"Okay, sounds good." Jolie stifled a huge yawn as her body begged for sleep.

"I heard that yawn." Hank's deep chuckle washed over her. "Good night."

“Good night.” Jolie disconnected and put the phone on her nightstand. Elation and giddiness unlike any she’d experienced in a long time had a delicious shiver traveling down her spine. She had a date with a wonderful man. Suddenly, the world seemed full of promise.

Chapter Ten

Hank couldn't believe it. The fates seemed to have conspired against him. Oh, he had the tickets in hand for a wonderful first date with Jolie. He'd booked a reservation at one of the poshest restaurants. He had everything planned. Jolie had insisted on driving herself, instead of him picking her up. That had pricked a bit at his idea of a romantic evening, but he'd caved on the point.

Now it looked as if he'd have to cave on the entire date. Elsa was singing tonight and the substitute babysitter he'd hired had come down with a nasty stomach virus. He knew she wasn't making it up—it had affected a few other employees, as well. While the Nolter was prepared for dealing with ill employees, Hank wasn't.

He had no babysitter to fall back on. He'd tried Jolie on her cell phone, but he'd gotten voice mail each time. When she arrived, he'd have to tell her the date was off. He couldn't leave Ethan and Alli home alone.

He glanced at his watch and groaned in frustration. His first date was a bust. Luckily the kids were in their rooms and couldn't see how upset he was. It wasn't their fault.

A light knock sounded and Hank strode to the door. He

pulled it open and Jolie stepped inside. Damn, she was gorgeous. He couldn't believe he'd have to let her down.

Branson's shows weren't necessarily something you had to dress to the nines to attend. But Jolie looked lovely in a pair of black pants, flats and a lime-green sweater set. He'd dressed in slacks and a dark blue dress shirt.

"Hi," he said. She turned and smiled, and Hank's heart pounded. "You look beautiful," he told her.

"You don't look half-bad yourself." When he didn't smile back at her light compliment, her forehead creased slightly. "Is something wrong? Were you unable to get the tickets?"

"Oh, I got them," Hank replied. He jerked a hand through his hair, feeling incompetent. "I did try to call you—I left a voice mail."

"I turned my cell phone off. I didn't want to be disturbed. So what's going on?"

"I don't have a babysitter. I've tried everyone I can think of. I'd use the hotel's service, but it's full."

At that moment Alli popped out of her room and scampered up to Jolie. "Hi! You look so beautiful. Is tonight your date with my dad?"

"It is."

"Can I come?" Alli asked, her eyes hopeful.

"Alli…" Hank began.

"If you were going to go on a date with us, where would you go?" Jolie asked.

"To a magic show!" Alli proclaimed.

"She was watching a special on TV last night," Hank explained.

Alli didn't seem to hear him, or if she did, she ignored him and continued, "Then I'd go ride some of the go-karts out on the strip. Those look cool! I've been dying to try them."

"You have?" Jolie asked. She set her purse on a table. "What about food? It's five o'clock. Almost dinnertime."

"Snow cones and ice cream."

"You'd need to eat something real, as well." Jolie winked at Hank. He had no idea where Jolie was going with this. "What about skipping go-karts and riding roller coasters, instead?"

"I like those," Alli said.

"Good. Then it's settled. Go get your brother and we'll go to Silver Dollar City."

Silver Dollar City was a local amusement park that had been around long before Branson had developed into a theater mecca. "You're overdressed," Hank protested.

"I'll change," Jolie said easily. "I happen to have stopped by my parents' house yesterday. Some of my things got switched with my sister's over Memorial Day weekend, so we swapped them back. I have everything I need in the car. So go change."

"You'd do this?" Hank asked.

Jolie stepped forward. "I said yes to a date with you. Your children are a part of you. Now go get ready."

Hank marveled at how special Jolie truly was as he went to change.

THREE HOURS LATER, Jolie wondered what she'd been thinking.

Not that she wasn't having fun. She was having a blast. But roller coasters and other rides had tiny seats. She'd been pressed up against Hank all night, thigh to thigh, arm to arm. In a theater she'd have at least had a seat divider between. With every turn of the rides, g-force had her connected with him. In fact, once when motion had brought their faces mere inches apart, Hank had closed the distance and given her a light kiss before the ride had spun them off. Today had made her more physically aware of Hank than ever.

She wanted more kisses and whatever might follow them.

His touch teased when he loosely held her hand as the foursome went off in search of ice cream and snow cones.

"Having fun?" Hank whispered in her ear.

"Most definitely," she replied.

"You know I wanted you to myself," he said.

"I know, but look how happy they are." Ethan and Alli raced on ahead, the ice-cream shop in sight.

He paused and turned to face her. "You do want alone time with me, too, don't you?"

His eyes reflected his uncertainty. "Yes," Jolie told him, the word full of conviction. "I adore your children, but I wouldn't be here just for them. I'm here because of you. I want to get to know you."

"Good." Hank leaned over to give her another quick kiss before they followed Ethan and Alli into the shop.

Jolie thought about Hank's words later as she helped him tuck Ethan and Alli into bed around midnight. The kids fell asleep almost immediately and she joined Hank on the couch.

"Not quite the date I'd imagined, but thank you," he said. "It was wonderful and meant a lot to them."

Jolie touched the side of his face with her palm. He must have shaved that afternoon, because his skin was still smooth. "I didn't do it for them."

With that she edged closer, and Hank met her halfway. The kiss started sweetly and then grew more intense. Jolie felt a fire spread in her stomach and move lower. No doubt about it—she wanted him. He made her feel beautiful and cherished.

His touch made her ache for more. His fingers were slow

and steady, tentative almost, and she realized that Hank hadn't touched anyone like this in a long time. However, there was nothing unnatural about the way he cupped her breast through the T-shirt she'd changed into earlier. Then, made a bit bolder by the soft sigh she uttered, Hank pushed the scoop neck of the shirt lower and freed her breast from her bra for his appraisal. He ran two fingers over her and then his gaze locked with hers.

"May I?"

All Jolie could do was nod. She was on fire, and as he lowered his mouth to taste, his tongue did nothing to cool the building heat. He freed her other breast, the lowered bra and T-shirt giving extra lift as he moved his mouth over her.

Hank didn't let up until her body quivered under his touch and she sighed her satisfaction. But instead of continuing, he covered her back up. "The kids," he whispered.

"I understand," Jolie replied. Without the privacy of a locked door and with two children sleeping down the hall, this was as far as they could go tonight. As it was, it had been a major step, especially for Hank. Jolie knew he'd touched no one since his wife's death. And making love on a first date would be rushing things. "Thank you."

"I should be thanking you. You've made me feel alive again." He kissed her lightly on the lips. "You are very special to me and I'm not afraid to admit it."

"Good," Jolie said, a tad frightened herself. She'd had so many failed relationships.... She shoved the negativity from her mind. "I should probably get going."

"You could use the spare bedroom."

"It's okay. I'd rather not. It would send the wrong message."

He nodded and helped her to her feet. "Will I see you before the wedding?"

"Can we play by ear? It's a crazy week with family events. Even tomorrow I have some silly shower related to the wedding."

"That's fine. I have tons of business meetings this week. It was probably wishful thinking. However—" he pulled her into an embrace "—you and I will talk. I'll call you tomorrow."

"Perfect," Jolie replied, letting him sweep her away into one final, deep kiss.

"SO HOW DO I LOOK?" Hank turned to face his two children, who were sitting on his bed watching as he dressed for the wedding.

"I think you look beautiful," Alli said.

"Beautiful is not a word you use to describe a guy!" Ethan shouted.

"I think it's fine," Hank interceded before the situation escalated. Ethan was frowning and readying for a fight.

"See? I'm right," Alli said, sticking out her tongue at her brother.

"However, Ethan is also right," Hank finished. "Usually you don't say a guy is beautiful. Especially if you're a guy. But girls, it's fine if they say it."

"Oh," Alli said, deflating a little. "You say Jolie's beautiful," she accused Ethan.

"I think she is," Ethan responded. "How about you, Dad?"

Hank gave himself another glance in the mirror. He'd chosen a dark blue suit, a white shirt and striped tie to wear to the wedding. All were custom-made at a store in Chicago. He hoped his admittedly beautiful date would approve of his appearance. "I think Jolie is very pretty."

"But not as pretty as Mom," Alli said.

"Very few women are as pretty as your mom was, but I think Jolie's one of them. She just has dark hair. And you like her."

Alli conceded the point. "I like her a lot. That's why I don't know why we can't go with you today."

"Because the wedding is for grown-ups only and you and Ethan went with us on our date last weekend. You know we'd take you otherwise."

"I know," Alli said.

Hank adjusted the knot on his tie and kissed the kids good-night before leaving them in the capable hands of the now healthy babysitter. The valet had the Lexus ready and soon Hank had reached Jolie's townhome. As he raised his hand to knock on her front door, it opened.

"Hi," she said, moving aside so he could enter. The door hid her from view and he couldn't tell what she was wearing.

"Hey," he said, trying not to sound like a teenage boy on his first date. He turned to face her as she shut the door, and his jaw dropped. "Wow."

She smiled tentatively. "I guess that's a good reaction."

"Very much. You look lovely." That was an understatement. She'd chosen a sleeveless V-neck sheath dress in pale pink. The color suited her, giving her a soft glow. She was beautiful even without makeup, but she'd applied some today and the effect was to make her eyes wider and her pouty mouth more kissable.

"You look great yourself," Jolie said.

He had the sudden urge to test just how kissable those lips were and forget about leaving altogether.

She glanced at the gold watch on her wrist. "We should probably get going."

Reluctantly, he reached past her for the doorknob, wishing they could stay and resume what they'd started last weekend. "If you're ready."

"As good as it gets," she replied, and soon they were on their way to the church.

"Who are these people again?" he asked.

"My cousin Alison is marrying some hotshot entertainment lawyer." Jolie dug in her small white bag and pulled out an invitation. "Simon Schuster."

"Sounds like a book company," Hank said.

Jolie grinned. "Hadn't thought of it that way, but you're right. Alison's a junior lawyer and supposedly it's a match made in partnership heaven. My aunt's ecstatic. Simon comes from money."

"And that's important?"

"To her it is. My mom and her sister are polar opposites. Her sister is all about appearances. She married a banker and my mom married a school superintendent. You can see the social dilemma. They aren't that close. Mom's closer to everyone in my dad's family."

"Ah," Hank said. "The reception should be nice, though."

"They spent enough. It's an open bar."

"Helps my bottom line and profit margins come quarterly-report time." Hank laughed, exiting the highway at the turnoff for the church.

"We'll be sure to drink up, then," Jolie replied with a wicked grin. "After all, you don't have to drive anywhere."

"I have to take you home, remember?"

"Not if we imbibe too much. My mom got a room for her and Dad."

Hank shook his head. "I don't think so. If we get tipsy, you won't be sleeping with your parents."

"No?" She slanted a glance at him as the flirting escalated to another level. She'd thought of his caresses all week.

"I think I could find you a room," he said.

"What if the hotel is all booked up?"

"Oh, I believe I know a place where you could crash."

"You do?" she asked, trying to sound innocent.

They'd reached the church, and Hank parked the sedan. "Yes. You do things to me and that dress isn't helping matters."

"Ah, I see," she said, pleased. It had taken an entire day to find something suitable, yet sexy, to wear to the wedding and reception. Since her mother always maintained it wasn't appropriate to wear black to a wedding, Jolie had ruled out her one little black dress and hit the mall.

She'd found this dress at the fifth store she'd tried.

Hank reached over and touched her hand. "I guess we better head inside."

Jolie sighed. "If I forget to tell you later, you're a saint for bringing me."

"It won't be that bad," he insisted. "Trust me."

"I do," she said, and with a smile, she let him lead her into the church, where they found her parents already seated. Jolie and Hank crammed in the pew beside Lance and his wife, Meg, and Clay and Lynn. Jennifer and her husband were there with her parents, and soon Bill and his wife arrived and rounded out the row. By the four-o'clock starting time, the church was packed and the ushers were seating the bride's grandparents and parents.

"Was your wedding like this?" Hank asked as the first of seven bridesmaids started down the aisle.

"No," Jolie said. "We did things on a much smaller scale and followed with a buffet at the local Knights of Columbus hall. We paid for everything ourselves, so we did everything on the cheap. We even married around New Year's so the Christmas decorations would still be up. Poinsettias were the flower of the day for all but the bouquets."

"Sounds wise."

"I guess. I was divorced less than three years later. I gave birth in December, Ruthie died in May and it took about six months to get all the paperwork finalized once we decided the following December that we didn't suit."

"I'm sorry," Hank said.

"I've moved on," Jolie replied, standing as the organist signaled the start of the wedding march, and soon cousin Alison came down the aisle in all her glory.

The actual ceremony lasted only twenty minutes. The reception began at six, which meant there was an hour and a half to kill.

"We're going to check in to the hotel," her mother said as the ushers began to dismiss the rows.

"We hadn't realized it was going to be this short." Clay touched his wife's elbow. "Any thoughts?"

"How about we go to the Nolter?" Hank suggested. "We can wait in the Starlight Lounge. It doesn't open until seven, so we'll have the place to ourselves. I can rustle up some snacks and beverages."

"That would be wonderful," Maudie said. "I think we'd all agree to that."

They followed the crowd to where the newly married couple received their guests in the church lobby.

"Jolie!" Alison said as Jolie stepped in front of her. "How good to see you! I'm so glad you could come."

"I wouldn't have missed it," Jolie said. She gestured. "This is my date, Hank Friesen."

"Hank, nice to meet you. You'll be at the reception, too?"

"That's the plan," Hank said easily as he shook her hand.

"Wonderful, we'll talk then," Alison said before turning to her next guests—more of Jolie's immediate family. Jolie moved on to her aunt and uncle, introducing Hank, and finally they were outside the church on the pavement in front of the steps.

"Okay, we survived that," Lance said as his wife punched him playfully. "The Nolter?"

"The Starlight Lounge is to the left when you go inside. We'll meet you there," Hank said.

"Sounds great." Maudie touched her husband's hand. "It's hot out here. Let's go."

Hank and Jolie walked toward his car. "That was nice of you, offering the lounge," she said once they got under way.

"It was that or my suite, and the kids are there. I'd rather keep today adults only."

"You have great kids."

"Yes, but I want a little one-on-one time with you," he admitted.

Jolie smiled. "So what was *your* wedding like?" she asked.

"Big. Amanda was an only child, so her parents pulled out all the stops. I don't remember much about it. Can't remember what I ate, what music the band played."

"Can you remember her face?"

Hank smiled wistfully and shook his head. "Only vaguely. Almost as if it was a dream."

"I'm sorry," she said.

He shook his head. "I can't wallow in regret. I've learned that. She gave me the most precious gift, in Ethan and Alli. But I'm ready to take my life off hold."

"I worry at times that you're rebounding," Jolie admitted. "Like you've come out of a fog, so whatever's in front of you is new and fresh. I worry that you've put me on a pedestal I'm doomed to fall from."

"I will admit it's different, dating now. But I love being with you, the real you, flaws and all. I'm very much looking forward to exploring this thing between us."

"Me, too."

"Good." Hank turned into the main entrance of the Nolter and handed off the car keys to the valet. He made a stop at the front desk, went behind into the back office and came back a few minutes later. "The lounge is ours. I let the lounge manager, Tony, know we'd be using it."

"How much will we owe you?" Jolie asked as they made their way to the lounge.

"Nothing. It's on me. We're good. Tell your family to drink whatever they want. I've ordered two appetizer samplers to tide us over." Hank took out a key ring and unlocked the doors.

"You are too kind," Jolie said, giving him a quick kiss.

"Flattery will get you everywhere. Another kiss and you can have whatever you want."

"Sounds perfect," Jolie said, brushing her lips over his. She would have lingered, but her family had arrived. Soon they'd commandeered two tables inside the lounge and were enjoying appetizers and drinks. At quarter after six they turned the room back over to Tony and his arriving staff and made their way to the grand ballroom, where Alison was hosting her reception.

"I probably shouldn't have had that wine," her mother said, giggling as they entered the ballroom. "Oh, isn't this nice?"

One whole wall of the ballroom opened to the atrium and the fountain. Waiters roamed the area carrying trays of wine, champagne and appetizers. A central bar served cocktails and nonalcoholic drinks.

"So, Hank, if you remarried, could you have the reception here for free?" Lance asked.

"Ugh! You are so insensitive. Ignore him," Meg said as they found their assigned seats. The tables seated ten easily, so all but Jolie's parents were at one table. The elder Tomlinsons were seated closer to the head table.

"Actually, I do get pretty good perks working here," Hank said. "Travel accommodations are always free for site managers, so a trip to Hawaii would be airfare and food only."

"I've never been there," Jen said. "We haven't been anywhere alone since we had kids. Oh, Six Flags, St. Louis, but that's only four hours away by car."

"Our showcase hotels are in New York and London," Hank told her.

"London would be wonderful, too," Jen said, then she turned her attention to the person announcing the arrival of the bride and groom. Dinner came shortly thereafter, and a little after nine the cake had been cut and dancing had started.

"Shall we?" Hank asked once the dance floor opened to everyone.

As a girl Jolie had felt gangly because of her height, but next to Hank she felt like a princess. The band played a slow number and Hank held her close. They moved in time with the music, shutting everything out. Jolie tried to remember if she'd ever felt this way with Reggie, but any comparison was irrelevant.

Hank bested everyone. He was perfect. He fit her. She fit him. It seemed too good to be true.

The song ended and he led her from the dance floor. The evening was so enchanting Jolie wondered if she would lose a slipper….

Alison might have been the one who'd gotten married, but this night ranked up there as one of Jolie's best ever. By eleven-thirty the party was still going strong. Out of her immediate family, only her parents had left.

The band played another slow number and Hank once

again drew Jolie into his arms. She leaned her head on his shoulder and let the music carry her away until she felt a tap on her shoulder. "We're going to head out," Lance said.

"You're okay to drive?" Jolie asked.

"Absolutely. Stopped drinking a few hours ago. I knew we had to get home by midnight for the babysitter."

"Okay, then." Jolie waved at Meg, who waited near the dance floor. The rest of her family left shortly afterward.

"I guess we should get going, too." Jolie sighed. She knew she didn't need to worry about Hank's sobriety. They'd barely stopped dancing long enough to have a sip of water, much less anything stronger.

"That would probably be wise," Hank said. "I'm going to need to drive you home so I can relieve the babysitter. Luckily for me she's part of the summer staff living at the hotel, so she only has a short walk."

"There are other staff who stay at the hotel?"

"We hire about a dozen college students each summer for various jobs. The education majors run the summer kids program and also babysit. It's called Camp Nolter. That's why we were in a bind last weekend. A bunch of people were sick."

"I never knew something like this camp existed."

"Not all hotels do it. We're somewhat similar to a cruise ship in how we approach Camp Nolter. We don't want our guests to be limited by having to return at a specific time to pick up their children."

"Ooh, I love it when you talk hotel," Jolie joked as Hank swept her into his arms. Reluctantly, he released her.

"Seriously, as much as I hate the idea, we have to go. The sitter is scheduled to be on duty tomorrow at 9:00 a.m."

"I should have just asked Lance or Jen to take me home," Jolie protested.

"Then we wouldn't have any alone time," Hank said as they left the ballroom. "I figured we'd do some old-fashioned making out in the parking lot, like teenagers or something."

Jolie giggled at the image. "I have a couch at my place we could use."

"Yes, but if I come inside, I'll never leave."

"Ah, the dilemma," Jolie said, catching Hank's hand as they walked through the lobby. "What to do? What to do?"

"You could stop tempting me," he told her as they waited for the valet to retrieve the car.

"Never," Jolie said, leaning over to kiss Hank.

"But you must," he said, not bothering to release her. Jolie liked the feel of his firm lower back against her palms. She hated that he wouldn't be able to stay tonight, but that was the way things worked sometimes.

Hank drove her home and they talked and laughed about the night's events until he pulled into the apartment-complex parking lot. He lowered the windows and shut off the ignition. The early-June night was like baby bear's bowl of porridge—just right.

"Kiss me before I walk you to your doorstep?" he asked.

"Absolutely," Jolie said, capturing his mouth with hers. She reluctantly pulled away several minutes later. "You have to go or you'll be late."

"We'll postpone this until later," he promised. Then he frowned. "Oh, I forgot. I'm visiting my parents next weekend. They called before I picked you up for the wedding."

"That sounds great," Jolie said, disappointed that she wouldn't see him.

"You could come with me."

"It's not too soon?" she asked.

Hank cupped her chin gently with his fingertips. "No. Could you go? I'd like you to meet them."

"Summer school's over daily by three."

"So would you go?" he clarified.

Jolie inhaled deeply. "Yes."

Hank kissed her again, his lips and tongue teasing hers. "Good," he finally said. Before his resolve left him, he gripped his door handle and pushed it open. Light flooded the car as he walked around to open Jolie's door. He went up the stairs with her and waited as she placed the key in the lock.

"I'll call you tomorrow," he said.

"I'd like that."

"Maybe we could grab a pizza if you're free."

"I should be," she said. "Call me around noon."

He ran a finger down the side of her cheek and she leaned into his touch. "I will. Good night."

"Be safe driving home," she said as they separated.

He kissed her one last time and then Jolie turned the key and stepped inside. She leaned against the closed door until she heard him drive away. She went to the balcony and walked outside. The lake far below was quiet, but everywhere the feel and smell of summer was in the air.

Her phone rang and she rushed back into the room to grab it. "What did you forget?" she asked.

"I forgot to tell you I had a great time tonight."

"Me, too." She suddenly realized that he'd called within a few minutes of leaving her after each date they'd had. "Sleep well."

"I'll dream of you," he teased, and then with another promise to call her tomorrow, he disconnected.

Jolie walked back to the balcony and shut the door before any bugs came inside and any more coolness from the air-conditioning escaped. She shut off the lights in all but her bathroom, where she assessed her appearance. He'd kissed away her lipstick. She touched her lips with a forefinger, remembering the feel of his mouth on hers.

Could this be it? She liked him. He touched her and her heart raced. She wanted more. She wanted to be close to him. She paused as she poured eye-makeup remover onto a cotton ball. If this relationship with Hank worked out, could she be a good stepmother to Ethan and Alli? The one time her child had needed her, she'd failed.

There was no guarantee she wouldn't fail again.

Chapter Eleven

Meeting Hank's parents wasn't nearly as scary as Jolie had thought it would be. They'd welcomed her with open arms, put her belongings in a guest bedroom and immediately turned their attention to their grandchildren, freeing Hank and Jolie to tour Springfield.

They'd had a long, leisurely lunch Saturday while Hank's parents took the kids shopping and out to a kid-friendly museum. Hank and Jolie spent the time talking and getting to know each other, but one thing remained unchanged—not being able to touch him more was driving her crazy. She knew Hank felt the same. They were ready for a continuation of what they'd started the night of their first date.

"You know, we could come visit the kids next weekend," Hank's mother said as they prepared to drive back to Branson on Sunday. "Harry wants to see that magician who's just starting his show. If you can get us tickets, we'll come down and stay with you. That way you and Jolie can have some alone time the night when we're not at the theater. I also promised Alli I'd take her to the *Titanic* museum."

Jolie felt a warm glow inside as she realized that through this gesture, Hank's parents were showing they accepted her.

"That could work," Hank said. "I know we don't have

anything planned. Let me check with the concierge and call you tomorrow."

"Well, maybe we'll see you next weekend, then. It was nice meeting you, dear."

"You, too." Jolie smiled. She liked Hank's parents. They'd welcomed her with open arms, unlike Reggie's parents who'd always been hypercritical of her.

Hank did indeed manage to get tickets, so the next weekend his parents came down. Friday night, Hank's parents took Ethan and Alli to a movie, and Jolie and Hank found themselves totally alone with no kids and no worries.

"Where are we going?" Jolie asked as they climbed into the car.

"I had Benson make reservations for us."

Jolie glanced down. She was in capris, sandals and a pink T-shirt. "I'm not really dressed to go anywhere fancy."

"You're perfect," Hank said. He wore tan Docker shorts and a navy, short-sleeved polo. "I asked for a place that's casual yet highly romantic. Amazingly, he knew of one."

The car began to climb into the hills around Branson, heading away from the lake, which appeared as a wash of blue far below. He turned onto an asphalt driveway, where a small white sign indicated they'd reached Hilltop Winery.

The drive in was about a quarter mile of twisting road, which ended at an old, Southern-style plantation home. "I didn't know this was here," Jolie said.

"They're mainly a bed-and-breakfast, but they also do one dinner seating. We're right on time."

He parked the car and they walked onto the front veranda. Others had gathered there, a few lingering near pitchers of iced tea or cold lemonade.

"Help yourself," a woman said, exiting the front door with a clipboard.

"Thank you. We're the Friesen party of two," Hank said.

"Excellent. Wait here until you hear the dinner bell." She made a notation with a pencil and moved on, greeting guests. The day was so mild and the view of the surrounding hills so beautiful that no one wanted to be inside, anyway.

"What would you like?" Hank asked, then went to the sidebar and poured Jolie the glass of lemonade she requested. There were a few sugar cookies sitting on a serving dish nearby and he popped one of those into his mouth.

Soon, the dinner bell rang and they all went inside. The dining room was huge, the ceilings at least twelve feet high. There was one long table in the center seating eight, and along the walls were other tables seating two or four. When everyone was seated, not one spot remained open.

"Popular," Jolie remarked.

"We can tour the gardens later if you like. The grounds don't close until ten."

"Seems like the ideal place for a honeymoon. Quiet and peaceful. Not chain-ish."

"You mean unlike the opulent honeymoon suite at the Nolter?" Hank teased.

"Exactly. Reggie and I went to some couples hotel in Jamaica for our honeymoon. It was nice, but overdone. I'd rather do subtle things. Hiking. Lying on the beach. Having privacy. They show you that on the brochures, but in reality other guests are only ten feet away."

A waitress brought them glasses of water. "Will you be having wine with dinner?" she asked.

"Yes," Hank said.

"Very good," she replied and then she disappeared.

"That's it?" Jolie asked.

"Part of the surprise," Hank said. "There's no menu. We

get whatever they're serving. Each course is paired with one of their wines."

"Sounds wonderful. I've never been anywhere like this."

"Neither have I, but I thought it would be a great date. Nothing to think about. Just eat, drink and get to know each other."

The waitress returned with two glasses of wine and a cheese tray. She also brought a menu card listing what would be in the five courses they were serving.

"I'm going to explode if I eat all this," Jolie said.

"We'll walk it off later," Hank promised.

The meal was leisurely and unrushed, and Jolie found herself with a sense of heightened anticipation. An hour passed before the roast-duck entrée appeared.

Once, she might have worried that she'd run out of things to talk about on a date, but she and Hank easily filled the time. She could claim it was the wine loosening their tongues, but in reality it was that they were so compatible. She'd never felt as comfortable with a man. He understood her, and better, she understood him. They trusted each other.

"You told me once that you wanted to buy a house. Aside from that, what is it you want most?" Hank asked.

"I'm not sure," Jolie replied. "I'd love to travel. As you know, I thought about taking a trip this summer, but life got in the way. Not that I've minded," she assured him.

"Me, neither," Hank replied. "Since coming to Branson, I think I may have found everything I want."

"What about climbing higher on the corporate ladder?"

"That's always been my goal, but my kids come first. I'd hate to move them again. A higher position would take me back to Chicago, which sort of defeats the purpose of our original move—to make a fresh start on our own. Don't worry, I'm not going anywhere yet."

Jolie relaxed. Her heart had skipped a beat when he'd mentioned moving back to Chicago. She had no desire to see Hank leave so soon after they'd started dating.

Coffee and mints followed dessert. Then Hank and Jolie took advantage of the weather and strolled the grounds. Discreet lighting illuminated the walking paths, and Hank held her hand as they enjoyed the fresh evening air. "So tonight was good?" Hank asked.

"I think when you get back you can tell your concierge he hit the jackpot. This is a rare find. I'd like to stay here someday. We only got to see part of the first floor, and I bet the rest of the house is just as fantastic."

The back of the menu card had given a brief history of the house. Apparently the bedrooms were decorated in period furnishings. They walked past a lily pond and a while later a swimming pool that was set into the landscape as if it were a natural pond.

"Perhaps we can come here for a romantic getaway," Hank suggested.

They'd reached a small moonlit clearing. "I'd like that."

"So would I," Hank said before bending his head to hers. His lips were gentle and sweet. They stood there, silhouetted against the night, savoring the moment.

"What time do you have to get back?" Jolie asked.

"Sometime tomorrow morning."

"Then you could take me home and stay a while," she said.

He kissed her again, making his feelings about her suggestion clear without saying a word. On the drive to Jolie's town house they discussed local history and world events, but anticipation was almost a third person in the car.

She had the urge to tear his clothes off the minute they stepped through her door. Instead, she offered him a drink, but he turned that down, took her hand and led her to the couch.

"I want to be with you," he said, "but I need to be sure we're ready. Making love changes things."

"Are you ready?" she asked.

Hank nodded. "When Amanda died, she urged me to love again. But I knew that didn't mean indiscriminately or cheaply. I'm not with you because of lust. I want you to know that. I care about you a great deal."

She kissed him gently. Now that they'd chosen their path, he deepened the kiss. His right hand wove into her hair, and his left arm circled her waist and pulled her closer. His lips teased and nipped, trapping her bottom lip in a soft suckle before releasing. His tongue traced her flesh and Jolie's mouth parted, allowing him to slip inside.

The movement sent desire racing through her. Kissing Hank was an epiphany. She felt as if she'd come home, found something she'd been searching for her whole life. The best part was that there was more. They'd barely gotten started.

She concentrated on the passion growing between them. She ran her palms over the shirt he wore, her fingertips digging into the solid chest beneath.

He moved his hand from her hair and used a finger to trace her jaw.

"You are so perfect," he whispered as his lips brushed her cheeks and her eyelids. "You're doing things to me."

"Awesome things," Jolie agreed.

He groaned and brought his mouth back to hers.

She reveled in the beauty of the moment, then stood and wordlessly led him to her bedroom. She tugged up his shirt so she could touch him without barriers. His skin was smooth under her fingertips.

He ran his hand beneath her T-shirt, and massaged her lower back. She'd gone a lifetime without a touch as gentle as this.

They sat on the bed and his hands moved to her breasts, cupping them through the fabric of her bra and then sliding underneath to pebble her nipples between his fingers. She inhaled sharply, her legs clenching. Then she leaned back against the comforter as Hank's lips replaced his fingers.

"You are so beautiful. I want to taste you all over," he whispered before gently nipping one rosy peak.

A wave overtook her and her entire body trembled. "That feels so good," she gasped.

"I'm glad," he said with a mischievous wink, and Jolie allowed her head to fall onto the pillow. Her T-shirt and remaining clothes vanished and his fingers moved to explore the sensitive places between her legs. He took his time, as if memorizing the feel of her.

She was so wet, and he rubbed his fingers over her and into her, sending her into slivery fragments.

Time slipped away, seemed to stop as Hank refused to rush or worry about his own needs. Instead, he replaced his fingers with his tongue and drove her over the edge again.

"Jolie," he said, his lips brushing the inside of her thigh as her body quivered in the sweet aftermath. "What do you want? What can I give you?"

"All of it," she said, overwhelmed by the sensations he drew from her body. She'd never made love like this. "Everything."

She helped him shed his clothes and then they were skin to skin. She stroked him with her palm, wanting to let him experience the same pleasure he'd given her.

"I want you," she said, locking her gaze onto his.

And then he was above her and inside her, filling her completely. The sensation was one of coming home.

She lifted her left leg and wrapped it around his lower back as he began to move. His eyes had glazed slightly and her hands slid to the sides of his thighs. He let her set the pace, and as the pleasure of another orgasm began to build inside her, she raised her head and watched him, marveling at the beauty of the act and the strength of his body. Then she relaxed into the pillow and let her body race in time with his, crying out as they came together.

Afterward he lay with her, still joined, and she was secure in his arms as he planted kisses along her jaw.

"You okay?" he asked.

"Wonderful," Jolie said, snuggling closer. "I've never…"

"Me, neither," he said. "It's like the first time, and that's not a cheesy line." He held her tenderly and smoothed out her hair. "It's as if the world is new again. As if a fog has lifted. You've made me feel alive."

They cuddled closer. The food had made them full, the wine mellow, and the lovemaking sleepy. Within moments, they'd both drifted off, tucked tightly together.

HANK ROSE just before dawn. His body clock usually had him up at six, anyway, but today he wanted to get home before Ethan and Alli woke up. He slid out of the bed and gazed down at Jolie. She needed her sleep. After they'd first made love they'd slept for a few hours and then one of them, he wasn't sure who, had stirred and they'd ended up making love all over again.

The night had been a slice of pure heaven. He reached over and pushed a strand of Jolie's hair away from her face. She wrinkled her nose, but didn't wake. That was probably good. She was naked beneath the sheet, and already Hank's body craved more. She'd given him the most precious gift last night. Her touch had healed his heart and his soul. He'd felt complete for the first time in years.

While he hated slipping out like a thief in the night, they'd discussed this after their third time. She'd said she would wake up, but he didn't want to disturb her. She must be exhausted. She'd worn him out, that was for sure. He ached in all the delightful ways he'd long forgotten.

Once he was dressed, he reached down and adjusted the covers. He'd call her in the afternoon. He'd fallen into the habit of talking to her daily, and he couldn't imagine doing otherwise. Besides, he had an upcoming work function he wanted her to attend.

He strode through her darkened apartment, almost reaching the door, when he heard her call his name.

Jolie walked down the stairs wrapped in a sheet, her hair tousled. "Hey. Are you leaving?"

"Yeah. I didn't want to wake you."

"You didn't at first, but then I realized you were gone. What time is it?"

"A little after five," he said, moving to stand next to her. "I'm going to sneak back home like a naughty teenager." He grinned. "Of course, everyone's sleeping so it's unlikely anyone noticed I wasn't there all night. But I want to be home when Ethan and Alli wake."

"As you should be," she said, and gave him a light kiss. "Go."

"Going," he responded, but was unable to resist capturing her lips again. Finally he groaned and dragged himself away. He heard her throw the lock behind him, and moments later he saw a curtain move as she watched him make it safely to his car.

Despite the disjointed sleep, Hank was wide-awake as he drove home. The June morning was crisp as the sun began to peer over the horizon. He lowered the windows and let the fresh air flow through. All around him the world came to life.

He smiled to himself and inhaled deeply. This sense of fulfillment was more than that of a man ending celibacy. It was the feeling of finally embracing life again. He laughed at this revelation, cranked up the stereo and sang off-key and loudly all the way home.

IT WAS AROUND ten-thirty when Jolie finally climbed out of bed. She groaned and headed into the bathroom. She'd forgotten she had a family brunch at Bill's house at noon.

She arrived after the event began, but not so late that anyone noticed. Still, Jen's razor-sharp eyes narrowed as if she recognized something had changed with her sister, and she cornered Jolie later that afternoon.

"So how was meeting the parents for the second time?" she asked.

"Great. They're wonderful people. Ethan and Alli really like spending time with them."

"And you?"

"I like them, too. Hank definitely takes after his dad, who still has all his hair."

"That's good. They say baldness is genetic. I'm glad my hubby's kept his hair. And his stamina." She winked.

"Jen, TMI," Jolie said, meaning too much information.

"Stop blushing. Please. It's not as if you don't know what sex is."

"Yeah, but I don't want to picture you having it," Jolie said with a grimace.

"Well, are *you* having it?" Jen shot back. Then, seeing Jolie's deepening blush, she shouted, "Oh, my God, you are!"

"Keep your voice down," Jolie hissed. "The last thing I need is my entire family discussing my sex life."

"I'm assuming it's Hank."

"Who else would it be?" Jolie demanded.

"Just checking," Jen said with a shrug.

"Jen! You are impossible!" Jolie tried to keep her voice below a shout. Her sister merely laughed.

"You have to give me some details," Jen said. "If you do I'll share a secret."

"It had better be good," Jolie said, swallowing a yawn. She smiled to herself remembering who was to blame for her lack of sleep.

"It's the best kind of secret… I'm expecting! I'm about ten weeks and we haven't told anyone yet. We plan to make the announcement later today. I'm going to give Mom and Dad that dozen." Jen realized her blunder. "Oh, God. I'm sorry, Jolie."

"No, it's okay," Jolie said. "It's getting easier. We don't need to forget my daughter—let's focus on the living. I'm so thrilled for you."

"Are you sure?" Jen asked.

"Absolutely." Jolie threw her arms around her sister, hugging her tightly.

"So enough about me and my insane decision to incubate a third kid. With my luck it'll be twins and I'll add three and four to my already chaotic household. Tell me about Hank. I want details."

"Did you ever hear of the Hilltop Winery?" Jolie asked.

Jen frowned. "It's a really exclusive bed-and-breakfast, right? You went there?"

"For dinner," Jolie explained. "Then we went to my place and we…well… You know."

"Where do things stand now?"

"He'll call me later. But he's not about to declare that he loves me and wants to marry me. We haven't been seeing each other that long."

"I don't think love depends on how long you've been together. You know when you know."

"Perhaps, but I don't have a track record for picking winners. So I'm not rushing into anything just because the lovemaking's great."

Jen arched an eyebrow in silent query and Jolie spilled, "Okay, phenomenal. Best ever. But that doesn't mean anything except we have dynamite chemistry. Besides, we're both busy with our own lives, and he has the kids to consider."

"You don't think you'd be a good mother to them?" Jen asked, clearly horrified that her sister could believe such a thing.

"I wasn't a very good mother before."

Jen sighed and wrapped her arms around Jolie. "Sweetie, that was an accident, a freak of nature. There was nothing you could have done."

"I could have woken up. Checked on her. Done CPR."

"You couldn't watch her twenty-four hours a day. You had your child placed in the crib properly. You did everything right."

"I tell myself that," Jolie said, "but sometimes I just can't accept it."

"Does Hank know about Ruthie?" Jen asked.

Jolie nodded. "I told him. He understands. He lost his wife to cancer. Sometimes things just don't go the way you plan."

"So stop planning. Let this relationship develop. I suspect Hank isn't going to let you out of his life soon."

"No, nor me him, but what if something happens? It just does in my world. I don't know why."

"Is that what you're afraid of?"

"Yes," Jolie admitted, allowing her insecurities to surface. "I've been hurt so many times before. I don't want to set myself up to lose again. Or to hurt someone else."

"Life doesn't come with guarantees."

"I know that," Jolie said. "But, damn it, I want one. I know I won't get it, but I want it."

They sat there for a few moments until Jen asked, "Do you think he wants more kids?"

"We haven't discussed it."

"Do *you* want more kids?" Jen asked.

"I'm not sure. What if I lost another child? I couldn't take it." A tear formed and Jolie angrily brushed it away.

"You've got a lot of questions to answer."

"Yes, and none of them are easy. It's like a minefield. Every time Hank and I get closer, more questions arise."

"You should talk to the man. Find out what he wants. Maybe you two can just have good sex for a few years. Maybe you'll fall in love and get married. You can raise Ethan and Alli and travel the world once they're in college. Or, if it's what you both want, you can have a child together. Lots of guys in Hank's age bracket have kids. Heck, they have them when they're sixtysomething. You hear about celebrities doing it all the time."

"Their wives are usually thirty years younger."

"So? Big deal."

But it *was* a big deal, Jolie thought later. Hank was perfect for her. But how many times had something that had at first seemed wonderful self-destructed for one reason or another? Everyone else in her family was happily married, but the bloom had been off the rose of Jolie's marriage quite quickly. Even after her divorce her luck hadn't improved. She'd start dating someone, and then poof, it'd be over.

With Hank she felt promise, hope, something beyond the best sex of her life. But she was uncertain and a bit scared about what the future would hold. What if he wanted more kids? What if he wanted to marry her?

Was she ready for those things? Part of her clamored yes, yes! Another part wanted to put her tail between her legs and run.

Jolie liked immediate answers. She wanted life clearly mapped out, in a very precise linear fashion. She liked patterns, things that were easy to read and understood.

Yet her relationship with Hank was a puzzle she couldn't solve.

So Jolie had to float along, let the days unfold one at a time. If she tried to rush, she'd make horrible missteps, and the fragile fledgling relationship between her and Hank was too precious to risk.

Chapter Twelve

By the middle of July, Jolie still had no answers. Life had fallen into a wonderful, predictable routine. Hank called. They'd talk. They'd take the kids somewhere for dinner or, if it was the weekend, on an outing. They visited all the tourist traps. At night they'd wait until the kids were asleep and then Jolie would slip into Hank's bed and they'd make love until the wee hours of the morning. She'd always make sure to leave before Ethan and Alli woke up and discovered her.

They'd spent the Fourth of July at the annual Tomlinson celebration; Ethan had told her he'd never seen a family that partied so much. She'd ruffled his hair and sent him on his way.

She'd even agreed to attend Premier Hotel's annual recognition dinner in Chicago this coming weekend, the last weekend of July. The four of them had flown to St. Louis and then caught another flight to the Windy City. Hank had arranged for the kids to stay with Amanda's parents. He'd reserved a suite at the Premier Michigan Avenue for himself and Jolie.

Now she was in the suite, waiting with Ethan and Alli for their grandparents. Hank was downstairs at a meeting, but he'd planned to be back before Sylvia and Ross arrived. However, it was almost five, and Hank hadn't yet reappeared.

"Don't worry," Alli said, obviously sensing Jolie's nervousness. "My grandparents will like you."

Jolie wasn't so sure about that, but she kept her negative thoughts to herself. "Are you excited about seeing them?"

"I've missed Grandmother and Grandfather," Alli said with a nod. Then she paused. "But I like living in Branson. I didn't like living there at first, but now I have friends."

"Me, too. Branson rocks. I got to go Jet Skiing!" Ethan said, his fingers working the controller for the video game he was playing.

"Yes, you did," Jolie said. Some of the friends Ethan had made during summer school had boats and personal watercraft, and Ethan had been a frequent guest. "I think this move has been really good for all of you."

Jolie truly believed that. There was a new maturity and confidence to the twins. Alli had come out of her shell, and she'd met another girl her age who also lived at the hotel. The girl's family was relocating from Memphis, and they were waiting to move into one of the newer houses under construction within the Nolter Elementary school district. Alli's new friend would be in fifth grade with her in August, which was a good thing, since the girls had become pretty inseparable.

Aside from boating, Ethan had joined the swim team and had placed in a few freestyle races. The coach had already provided Hank with information for the fall indoor season, and Ethan was excited about continuing.

So far the other shoe hadn't dropped on her relationship, but Jolie refused to let her guard down. She knew how much Hank cared, even though he'd never said *I love you.*

She also knew her own heart. She'd fallen deeply in love with the man and his children. She couldn't imagine life without them.

She took a breath. Maybe this weekend was the last big test. She'd meet Ethan and Alli's maternal grandparents. She'd meet all Hank's bosses and fellow hotel managers. The question was, would she live up to Amanda?

HANK GLANCED at his watch and mentally cursed. If this meeting didn't end soon, Ross and Sylvia would be at the suite before him.

He stilled his fingers, which were about to make an annoying staccato on the boardroom table. His bosses were impressed. While all the Premier Hotels were doing well, the Nolter had seen a fifteen percent revenue increase since Hank's arrival. They'd just entered the peak summer tourist season, and already bookings for the winter holidays were above projections, the spa-package reservations double what they'd been a year ago.

Hank hadn't realized the Nolter's special challenges until he'd arrived in Branson.

The town sat near three lakes. In contrast to the strip's glitz, most of Branson was laid-back and casual. It wasn't a high-end shopping mecca like New York or Chicago. Unlike Lake of the Ozarks, within its million-dollar homes, jet-set clubs, six-figure Scarabs and cabin cruisers, Table Rock Lake was quieter and more middle-class-family oriented. The Nolter, the most expensive hotel in Branson, had to justify its price tag. Five stars didn't necessarily mean much to people hanging out in fishing or pontoon boats.

Thus Hank had worked to position the Nolter differently. He still wanted the aura of luxury, but he wanted it to feel less exclusive, so that more travelers chose it over budget class or midrange lodgings.

He checked his Rolex again. Ross and Sylvia were rarely late for anything, and he knew they'd be on time to pick up their beloved grandchildren. Hank tried to catch Peter's attention. But the vice president of Premier Hotels was preoccupied with watching the PowerPoint presentation.

They'd arrived in Chicago at ten in the morning for the twelve-thirty meeting. Ross and Sylvia had asked to take the kids immediately, but Hank wanted to be present for the swap. That way he'd put them off until five-thirty. Jolie, who'd visited Chicago once before, had taken Ethan and Alli shopping at the Navy Pier, and done the mandatory trip to the John Hancock building observatory. Hank was envious—no matter how many times he enjoyed the view from the building's ninety-fourth floor, one thousand feet above street level, he always saw something different.

He grimaced with impatience as the meeting began to wind down. Agitation consumed him. He wanted to be there, to support to Jolie when she met Amanda's family. He knew this had to be difficult for her.

He wasn't going to be on time.

THE KNOCK on the door had Ethan whooping. Jolie groaned. Hank had assured her the meeting would be over at five. It was five-twenty and he still hadn't showed. As he had a key card, she was certain the knock belonged to—

"Grandmother and Grandfather!" Ethan shouted. He threw the door wide and two people who appeared to be in their midsixties stepped inside. The woman opened her arms, and Ethan gave her a big hug. Alli had reached them, and her grandfather gathered her into a bear hug.

"My, you've gotten tall," he complimented. "Turn around and let me get a look at you."

Alli puffed up and gave a little spin. "I grew two inches! I'm even taller than Ethan."

"Not by much," Ethan said. "Jolie says boys grow slower than girls."

"Her brothers did," Alli filled in helpfully.

Amanda's parents stepped forward into the suite and Jolie wiped her hands on her shorts. She hadn't changed since they'd come back from sightseeing. "Hi, I'm Jolie."

The silence was awkward as Sylvia and Ross stood there, summing her up. Admittedly, Jolie did the same. Sylvia stood five-two at the most, and Jolie felt like a giant beside her. Sylvia's hair was white and perfectly coiffed, as if she'd been in the salon that morning. Her taste ran to classic clothing, as did her husband's. Ross, in khakis, appeared as if he'd just stepped out of a posh country club.

"It's nice to meet you, Jolie," Ross said, breaking the silence. All three adults were aware of the two sets of watchful eyes witnessing the exchange. He reached out and she shook his hand, keeping her grip as firm as his.

"Yes, a pleasure," Sylvia said, her own handshake like a limp fish and fingertips only. She surveyed the suite. "Is Hank here?"

"I'm assuming he's running late," Jolie replied.

"Typical," Sylvia said.

"Not really," Ethan said in defense of his dad. "Not since we've been in Branson. Dad's really got his schedule under control. He says he can delegate more. Did he tell you I won a trophy for swimming?"

"*You* did, remember?" Sylvia said, turning to face her grandson. "I wish I could have been there."

"You should visit. We have an extra room!" Alli said.

"We will visit soon," Sylvia promised. "I've never been to Branson, but it sounds lovely."

"There are some awesome golf courses. I'm learning how to play," Ethan said.

Ross's eyes lit up. "Really? We'll have to go out and shoot nine holes tomorrow."

"Cool!" Ethan exclaimed. "Can I drive the golf cart?"

May I, Jolie mentally corrected.

"Now, are you two all packed?" Sylvia asked. "Since it's a special occasion, I made dinner reservations at the club."

"We never unpacked," Alli said.

"The club?" Jolie asked.

"Our country club. The four of us used to eat there all the time. I'll cook tomorrow night," Sylvia said.

"Lasagna?" Ethan asked hopefully.

"Absolutely."

"No one makes lasagna like my grandmother," Ethan said, and Jolie saw Sylvia's eyes tear up a little. Jolie could tell that Sylvia really loved and missed her grandchildren.

"We should get going if we're to make it on time," Sylvia said. "Are those your bags?"

"Yes," Alli answered.

"I'm sure Hank will be here any minute," Jolie said, not exactly certain how to handle the situation. It had to be odd for Sylvia, standing in the same room with the woman who, in a sense, was replacing their daughter.

"A minute won't hurt," Ross said, settling the matter, and sure enough, Hank arrived seconds later.

He draped his arm casually over Jolie's shoulders and gave her a quick kiss on the lips. "Sorry I wasn't here. The meeting ran late."

"It's okay," Jolie said, aware of Sylvia's scrutiny.

"Did you and the kids have a good day?" Hank asked.

"See my new doll clothes?" Alli held up her doll for her dad to see. "Jolie bought them for me."

"That was very nice of her," Hank said.

"I thanked her," Alli said with a nod.

"She did," Jolie confirmed.

"Good girl." Hank ruffled his daughter's hair and Alli beamed. He smiled at Ross and Sylvia. "You're both looking well."

"We went to Florida at the end of May," Ross said.

Sylvia gave a little cough. "How about we all catch up over brunch? Say noon on Sunday? We do need to get going. You know how traffic is."

"Jolie and I will take the train out Sunday if you can drive all of us to the airport."

"That will work," she said, and Hank bent down to give her a kiss on the cheek as she moved toward the door. "Thank you for letting us take them," Sylvia said.

"They've missed you," Hank replied, and within five minutes the suite was quiet again.

"So those're the in-laws," Hank said.

"They seem like nice people."

"They are, and you survived meeting them." Hank grabbed for the silk knot at the base of his throat and began tugging.

"Here, let me get that," Jolie said, stepping forward to loosen the tie. As she slid the knot down and away, Hank planted a kiss on her lips. "Hey, what's that for?" she asked.

"This has to be difficult for you." He circled her with his arms. "I just want you to know I'm with you all the way."

"I like the sound of that."

"Good," Hank replied, kissing her again. He glanced over her shoulder at his wrist.

"Am I boring you?" she asked.

"Not at all. I'm seeing how much time we have. We need to be downstairs at seven. That gives us an hour and fifteen minutes."

"I'd like a shower," Jolie said.

"How about we get a little more mussed up first?" Hank nuzzled her neck, then cupped her bottom. "How about we take a few minutes to check out the bed? They upgraded them just last month. Supposed to be heavenly."

"Bold, aren't you?" Jolie teased, her own desire heightening.

He slid his thumb under the hem of her shorts, brushing the soft skin of her inner thigh. "Uh-huh. Then a nice leisurely shower and..."

He gave up using words and lowered his mouth to hers. He changed the position of his hands, lifting her and carrying her into the bedroom.

Jolie sat on the bed and watched as Hank began to shed his clothes. They'd made love many times since the first night, carving out moments whenever they could. Every time was a revelation.

When they were both sated from their lovemaking, he leaned over her, kissing her mouth and her neck. Then he moved to lie on his back, one arm across his eyes, the other cradling her close. "Is it always going to be like this?" he asked.

"How?" she asked, nestling into his side.

"Perfect."

She snuggled closer. "I hope so."

"That's good enough."

They held each other for a while, enjoying the closeness. Finally Hank stirred. "I don't want to move, but we're going to have to."

"You promised me a shower," Jolie reminded him.

He shifted and propped his head up on an elbow. "I did, didn't I?"

"Mm-hmm," she said as his finger started tracing patterns on her chest. She slid out from his grasp and stood on the opposite side of the bed. "I'm heading there now. We can't miss the boat. I've never been on a dinner cruise."

"Go," Hank told her, sending her on ahead. Jolie wasn't too surprised when he joined her once the water started running. The luxury shower had multiple showerheads and easily enough space for two, and Jolie knew, as she and Hank made love again under the spray, that this would be one of her favorite memories.

The invitation called for black tie, so two weeks ago Jolie had phoned her cousin Alison for fashion advice. Alison had known the perfect store.

"You look lovely," Hank whispered in her ear as she gave herself one last glance in the mirror.

"You think?" She assessed the gown with a critical eye. The dark blue fabric shimmered. The neckline was higher in the front but plunged in the back, so she'd had the seamstress stitch in bust support; with her back bare, there was no way she could wear a bra. The dress came with a matching stole, and Jolie even had blue, one-inch heels.

"Yes, I think," Hank said. He slipped his hand into his tuxedo pocket and brought out a black jeweler's box. "However, this might help."

He opened the box, revealing a silver-and-diamond necklace and matching earrings.

"I can't accept these," Jolie said.

He chuckled. "As much as I'd like to give you these, I can't. I'm cheating. They're on loan."

"Okay. Good. I… It would have been too much. So, a loan. Perfect."

Hank unclasped the necklace and placed it around her neck. The hairs on the back of her neck prickled as she felt the gems' weight. Hank then handed her the box and she swapped her earrings for the ones that matched the necklace.

They made it downstairs by seven, moving across the lobby to where a group of women in evening finery waited with men wearing tuxedos. "They'll love you, so relax and have fun," Hank encouraged her.

"I'll try," she said, glad she'd spent a small fortune on the dress. Hank made introductions, and Jolie worked on memorizing names.

"This is Peter and his wife, Claire," Hank said, introducing Jolie to the last couple. "Peter has been my friend and mentor for as long as I've worked for him."

"It's a pleasure to meet you," Peter said, and something about his jovial manner made Jolie like him instantly.

When they reached the boat, Jolie and Hank were seated with Peter and Claire for dinner, and although the couple had known Hank for more than twenty years, Jolie never felt left out of the conversation. If anything, she learned more about the man by her side.

"I hope you like to travel, Jolie, because it's one of the greatest perks," Peter said over dessert.

"I do have summers off," she said. "But I often teach summer school."

"So have you ever thought of living anywhere besides Branson?" Peter asked.

"My family is there," she replied. "Branson's home."

"Jolie's a twin," Hank said, deftly changing the subject. He'd draped his arm across the back of her chair.

"My brother Lance and I are a bit like Ethan and Alli in our temperaments," Jolie supplied.

"How are Ethan and Alli?" Claire asked, and conversation

drifted to the kids for a few minutes before Jolie excused herself to use the restroom. To her surprise, Claire joined her.

"We have to go in pairs," Claire joked as they walked toward the restroom. "Besides, this will give Peter time to talk with Hank privately."

"They don't have time during work?" Jolie asked.

"Not lately. Peter's making noises about finally retiring. He's been hemming and hawing for years, but I think he's finally serious. I know my husband. He'll pick a date and that will be that. When he does, there's a VP spot open. I think that's what he wants to talk to Hank about."

"Oh," Jolie said, not sure how to respond. Once each woman had used the facilities and washed up, they resumed the conversation while retouching their makeup.

"Peter's always wanted Hank to be in the upper echelons of the company. He's done so well with the Nolter that, logically, putting him in charge of other managers could only benefit them and Premier overall."

"I'm sure Hank is capable," Jolie said, putting her lipstick back in her clutch purse.

"Hank would do great. But there's a catch. He'd have to move back to Chicago to be in the home office. Peter doesn't do a lot of traveling—the managers come to him—but it's still a very hands-on job."

"I'm sure Hank will make the right decision," Jolie said, shaken by the thought that Hank might move. Being the vice president would be a huge step in Hank's career. Jolie suddenly had doubts about how permanent Hank's move to Branson was.

"You can teach anywhere, right?" Claire was asking, and Jolie nodded.

"So if Hank does decide to return to Chicago, there's no reason you couldn't join him." Claire smiled. "Let me say that Peter and I are thrilled we finally got to meet you. After Amanda, I didn't think Hank would ever overcome his doldrums and love again."

"Thank you," Jolie said. "But I don't believe we're at that point."

Claire reached over and patted Jolie's arm. "He might not have said it yet, but all of his friends can see how he feels. He's in love with you and we think it's great. We're all happy for both of you, and now, after meeting you, I'll admit to being relieved."

"Relieved?"

"Oh, yes. We worried that some opportunist might grab him. Or someone not really suited to him. But I have a sixth sense about people. In all my sixty years, I've never been wrong. You're perfect for him. Now we should probably get back out there before they start thinking we fell off the starboard side or something."

"Good idea," Jolie said, awed and shaken by the conversation.

"YOU SEEMED QUIET after dinner," Hank said when they returned to their suite later that evening.

"Did you know Peter wants you to be the next vice president?" she asked.

"He's mentioned it before and then again briefly tonight. Why?" Hank didn't look too concerned.

"Claire told me in the bathroom. She said her husband's close to setting a retirement date."

Hank shrugged. "Peter's been saying that for the past few years, so I'll believe it when I see it. I think he'd be bored, anyway."

"Still, it's what you've been working toward," Jolie pressed.

Hank frowned. "Yeah, but that doesn't mean I'll jump at the job. I turned down a promotion to Seattle because Amanda didn't want to move. I have children to consider. And there's you."

"I can teach anywhere," she said, telling him the truth Claire had pointed out.

"Yes, but you're happy where you are," he said.

"So you'd consult me?" she said.

Hank stepped closer. He'd undone his cuff links, his bow tie and the first few buttons of his shirt. "Jolie, haven't you figured out how I feel about you? I wouldn't just up and leave without talking to you first."

"Okay," she said.

He moved to stand next to her and lifted her chin with his forefinger. "Look at me." She raised her eyes. "Better." His smile was gentle. "I guess I've been remiss in expressing myself. It's been a long time since I've started a new relationship, and I've forgotten some of the rules."

He took a breath, but didn't hesitate. "Jolie, I've fallen in love with you. I don't want you out of my life. I want you in it. I don't know if I'll ever be ready to remarry, but I didn't think I'd fall in love again, either, so I'm holding all my options open. If you'd asked me six months ago, I'd have laughed at the idea. But now…now the thought of love is very real. I love you."

"You love me," she repeated back to him, wanting to make sure she'd heard him correctly.

"Yes," Hank said. "I love you." He paused as he marveled at the words. "It's different from before. It's not the wide-eyed young love I had with Amanda. It's something more mature, perhaps even deeper. I know I'm botching the explanation, but you've captured my heart. Being without you is unthinkable."

His declaration had brought tears to her eyes, and he frowned, his forehead creasing. “Don’t cry, darling.”

“I’m happy,” she said, sniffling.

“With tears?”

“Happy tears,” she said, reaching up a hand to touch the side of his face. “I love you, too.”

“Then it is perfect,” Hank said. And as he captured her lips with his, Jolie realized Hank was right.

Chapter Thirteen

"Hey, Zane," Ethan greeted the valet as he jumped out of the car.

"Mr. Ethan," Zane said. "How was your trip to Chicago?"

"Great!" Ethan shouted, racing to the revolving doors and entering the hotel.

Jolie opened the passenger door to go after him, but Hank shook his head and shrugged. "It's fine. The bags will be brought up. He's just wired."

"Ethan's always wired," Alli said. "Grandmother said he's better, though. She told him he'd calmed down."

"That's good," Hank said. He hadn't had much of a chance to talk to his children about their visit. He hadn't seen them Saturday, as he and Jolie had had a company event and another company dinner. On Sunday they'd all had brunch with Ross and Sylvia, and then his children had been seated across the aisle during the flight home.

He'd worried that they'd return to Branson homesick for Chicago, but that hadn't happened. Instead, Sylvia and Ross had decided to come for a visit the next week. They would arrive on Thursday.

Ethan had worried at first about missing Jolie's nephew Skip's birthday party at the farm, but Jolie had insisted that two more would be welcome and the matter had been settled. Ross and Sylvia would stay with Hank and the kids in the suite.

"Ca— May I go on up, Dad?" Alli asked.

"Since your brother is probably halfway there, go ahead," Hank said, and Alli entered the hotel. Hank turned to Jolie. "Are you coming up?"

She shook her head. "Not tonight. I'm pretty tired and I'd be worried about falling asleep on the drive home if I stayed for a while. I'll see you tomorrow. Remember, my mom's giving Alli a piano lesson tomorrow and Ethan's been invited to Skip's."

"Bill's son."

"Right. Bill and his family live next door to my parents."

"Is Skip the one I need to get a birthday gift for next weekend?" Hank asked.

"Yes, but I'll take care of it, if you like. I know what Skip wants."

"Great! Give me the receipt and I'll reimburse you." The bellhop had loaded the luggage onto a cart.

"I need that one." Jolie pointed, and her suitcase was removed. "Zane, when you park Hank's car, will you bring mine around?"

"Certainly," the valet replied, and Jolie and Hank moved to the side as he climbed into the Lexus and drove off.

"I'm going to miss you tonight," Hank said, drawing Jolie close. "You won't be in my arms."

"I won't like it, either," she admitted. She leaned her head on his shoulder. "It's confusing for the kids if I stay over. That's far too domestic this soon. What if things change?"

"I know," Hank said. If he didn't have Ethan and Alli, he'd ask Jolie to start staying over. Give her a place to keep a toothbrush and store a few clothes. But children made relationships difficult. They changed a man's priorities. He didn't want a live-in girlfriend. He loved Jolie and knew she loved him and his kids. But he didn't want her to move in without everything being proper. The next step would be marriage.

And that was a step he wasn't yet ready to take. Not this soon. They needed to spend more time together. Really make sure their love would ripen into something that would last the rest of their lives.

He believed it would, but he couldn't risk the chance that he might be wrong. His children couldn't lose another mother.

Zane brought Jolie's car around, and Hank gave her a long kiss before she drove off. Then he went upstairs to where Ethan and Alli waited.

ETHAN HAD ALREADY retreated to his room and was playing a video game when Alli entered the suite. Wanting to speak with her brother, she knocked and walked in.

"Can't you see I'm busy?" Ethan asked.

"You're always busy." Alli scowled. "I wanted to ask you if what Grandmother said bothered you."

Ethan blinked and blasted a few more bad guys. "About what?"

"About Jolie being our new mom if Dad marries her."

"I think Jolie's great," Ethan said. "And her family's cool."

"Grandma's worried because Jolie never had kids before. What if she and Dad have kids? We'd have a baby in the house."

"It'd be like one of your dolls, only it would cry and poop. Sort of like Jolie's niece." Ethan's game chimed, indicating he'd reached the next level.

"Natalie," Alli filled in helpfully.

"She's always grabbing everything and sticking it in her mouth."

"She's one year old," Alli said.

"Whatever," Ethan said. "I'm oldest and that'll never change. So long as I don't have to change any diapers, it's cool."

"I think a baby would be okay," Alli said.

"Grandmother's just worried we'll forget Mom," Ethan said.

"I don't remember Mom that well," Alli admitted.

Ethan put down the game controller. "I don't, either."

"Do you think that's bad?" Alli's lips quivered.

Ethan shrugged. "I don't know. We have pictures. She'll always be our mom. But I like Jolie. Dad's happy when she's around. She's fun." Ethan started up the next level and went back to ignoring his sister.

Alli frowned and then left. She ran into her dad in the hall.

"Hey," he said. "Want to talk?"

Alli looked at her feet guiltily. "About what?"

Hank smiled at her and her worry eased until he said, "I overheard everything you just said to your brother."

HANK PUT HIS ARM around his daughter and guided her into her bedroom. The conversation he'd just heard had been enlightening. Alli sat down on her bed and he sat beside her. "You can talk to me about anything, you know," he told her. "I know you're worried that if Jolie joins our family, you'll forget your mom."

Alli nodded. "Grandmother says I will."

"Your grandmother lost her daughter and it's been hard on her." Hank had no idea how to break down such a complicated concept as death for a soon-to-be eleven-year-old. Sure, at its basic level death was simple—the person was there one day and forever gone the next. But losing someone to heaven was much more than that. There were stages of grief. Guilt at loving someone new. Fear of forgetting the one who died.

"You'll always have your mom with you even though she's no longer here on earth," Hank told Alli. He lifted a strand of her hair. "You look like her. You play piano. You have her eyes. All those little things keep who she was alive. You have her love deep inside your heart. She wanted you so much and was so happy when you were born. She loved you with all her heart."

"I miss her," Alli said.

"I do, too," Hank said.

"But you have Jolie," Alli protested.

"Yes, but that doesn't mean I'll ever stop loving your mom. She was a part of my life for a long time. She made me who I am today. She believed in me. She carried you and Ethan in her belly and gave birth to you two. Just because she died doesn't mean I'll forget her. But it doesn't mean I can't love someone else, either. Just like you haven't forgotten your old friends because you have new ones."

"What if you and Jolie have a baby?"

"Jolie and I haven't even decided to get married. I'd have to ask her first, and usually people date a while to make sure that they want to get married. Getting married is a big step."

"Was it big when you married Mom?" Alli asked.

"It was. Remember the photo album I showed you? All those wedding pictures? It was one of the best days of my life."

"So if you do marry Jolie and have a baby, you won't forget about me?"

Hank drew Alli into his arms. "Never. You're my girl. Do you think Jolie's sister Jen is going to forget her kids now that she's pregnant with another?"

"No," Alli said, giggling as Hank tickled her.

"Exactly. People have children because they love each other very much. It's not like toys. You don't have new kids because the other ones have gotten older."

"Good," Alli said.

"Someday you'll get married and have children and I'll be a grandpa," Hank said. "When you're thirty. That's a good age."

"Dad," Alli said, squirming now that he was giving her a hug. "A few of the girls in my class already have boyfriends."

Hank grimaced. "Really? I thought boys had cooties until at least high school. If not, they should get some."

"You are so silly sometimes," Alli chastised him. "I don't like anyone. I did like Jason, but he liked Sue."

"Those things happen," Hank said, realizing his children were growing up. "And no dating until you're twenty-eight."

"Dad," Alli said, laughing. "Sixteen."

"We'll see." His own laugh rumbled through the room. "So you're all okay now?"

"Yeah," Alli said. "Grandmother likes Jolie. She said she just doesn't want to see us get hurt."

"Neither do I." Hank crossed his heart. "And I promise that I will do everything to keep that from happening."

"You better. That's what a dad's supposed to do," she told him.

"I love you, sweetie," Hank said.

"Me, too," Alli said, giving him one more hug. Hank closed his eyes, memorizing the feel of his daughter's arms. Soon she'd be older and she'd think her dad was totally uncool. She'd resist hugging him.

"So you're okay with me dating Jolie?" he asked.

"You could marry her and that'd be okay," Alli told him. "She'd be a good mom."

"You love her?"

"Uh-huh," Alli confirmed.

"Good," Hank said. "Be sure to tell her that, okay?"

"You're weird, Dad," Alli said. Crisis over, she was ready to move on and do whatever girls did.

"Bedtime in a half hour," Hank told her. "Be sure to unpack your suitcase, too."

Alli rolled her eyes and exhaled. "Okay."

Hank stood and walked toward the door. He turned around and smiled at his daughter before he left. A sense of peace settled over him. He was no longer afraid, for the last unknowns had fallen into place. He knew what the future held. It was just a matter of time.

ROSS AND SYLVIA arrived Thursday afternoon. Instead of doing the ten-hour drive from Chicago, they'd chosen to fly, and Hank had cleared his schedule so that he could pick them up at the airport.

While everyone would fit into the Lexus, Hank had commandeered the hotel's limo and driver for the special occasion of Ross and Sylvia's first visit.

Thankfully Ethan and Alli had exhausted their curiosity before they reached the airport. They'd had to press all the buttons, put the divider up and down, change the channels on the satellite television and check out the contents of the small refrigerator. Hank had reprimanded them at first, but Buck, the Nolter's longtime driver, had only laughed and said it was okay as long as they didn't make him wash all the glassware. Instead, the kids drank directly out of the individual plastic soda bottles chilling in the fridge.

Jolie wouldn't join them tonight, but she'd be with them tomorrow.

Hank planned to talk to Ross and Sylvia that evening once the kids went to bed. He knew they weren't exactly thrilled with his dating, but it was what their daughter wanted. He was determined to make that clear. As for Friday he'd arranged a tee time for Ross and Ethan to play the Nolter's back nine. Sylvia wanted to visit the spa, and Alli had a playdate with her friend. Hank would be working, as usual.

Jolie would be out at her parents' helping her mother prepare for Skip's twelfth birthday party. As Hank had already learned, Tomlinson-family parties were a big deal. And since the farm had tons of amenities, just about every celebration occurred there.

His phone rang and, recognizing the programmed ring tone as Jolie's, he picked it up. "Hey, you."

"You there yet?"

"Arriving at the airport now," he told her.

"Ethan and Alli enjoying the ride?"

Hank glanced over. They were watching a cartoon. "Took a bit to settle down, but they're calm now."

"Good. What time will I see you Saturday?"

"We're planning on being out by one. Are you sure your family won't mind?"

"We love party crashers," Jolie said. "Ross and Sylvia don't have any grandchildren other than Ethan and Alli. They are more than welcome to join my family anytime. You've seen our reunions."

"I have, and they're incredible. Like you."

"Aw," she said. "Flattery will get you everywhere."

"I'll have to remember that." Hank could swear he heard her blush.

The limo drew to a stop in the hotel-shuttle lane. Hank, Ethan and Alli jumped out so they could meet Ross and Sylvia when they came through security. Buck would circle until they returned.

"We're here," Hank told Jolie.

"Okay. I'll talk to you later."

Hank pocketed the phone and followed the kids to the arrivals lounge. He tried to relax. Tonight's talk would go well. Ross and Sylvia might not like it, but they needed to understand that his relationship with Jolie was serious.

"YOU HAVE a lovely view," Ross said when Hank returned from tucking Ethan and Alli in. During the summer they were allowed to stay up until ten. And so, by the time they were in bed, the sky had darkened, the running lights of powerboats could be seen moving across the lake, and on the opposite shore, house lights beckoned. The Nolter had grown quiet for the night, but from the suite's balcony, they could hear a calypso band playing softly on one of the poolside terraces.

"Still, I think I preferred your house in Chicago," Sylvia said. "Not so high up."

Hank acknowledged that with a tilt of his head.

"So are you planning on buying a house?" Sylvia asked.

"I haven't gotten that far. We have life pretty easy here. Food, cleaning, no grass cutting."

"I gave that up this year," Ross said with a laugh. "Decided I had better things to do."

"You've carved out a life for yourself here," Sylvia said, ignoring her husband's comment.

From her tone, Hank could tell she remained conflicted. Part of her was glad the children had adjusted so well. But she had devoted five years to raising Ethan and Alli, embraced the challenge, and to be unneeded now…

"You did a great job with the kids, Sylvia. I couldn't have gotten this far without you."

"Thank you. I just wish you didn't live so far away. I miss seeing them daily."

"We needed to make a life for ourselves. It was time to move forward," Hank said. "I couldn't farm out my fatherly responsibilities any longer. I was managing, not parenting."

"You told me this before, but that doesn't make it any easier. Amanda would have wanted—"

"She would have wanted the three of us to be happy. To do that we needed a fresh start. We got that here. And just because we moved doesn't mean Ethan and Alli will forget you. Those kids love you. You saw how they ran to you today."

"I should be doing more," Sylvia insisted.

"You aren't their mother," Hank said gently. Ross reached over and held his wife's hand. "You filled that role for five years. You and Ross deserve more, as well. You did a great job, but it was time for me to stop leaning on you and take full responsibility for my children."

"But now they're spending so much time with Jolie," Sylvia protested. "They should be with me. I'm their grandmother. I'm family."

"Jolie may one day become part of our family, too. I'm not going to be a monk for the rest of my life. Some of Amanda's last words were that she wanted me to be happy. Jolie makes me happy."

"Are you marrying her?" Sylvia said.

"Not tomorrow," Hank said. "But I love her. I want her in my life. As we spend more time together, I hope we will move in that direction. I need for you to support that. Don't undermine her in front of the kids. No wicked-stepmother tales. Ethan and Alli don't need sheltering."

"So you say," Sylvia said. "I just don't want to see those kids get hurt. They've been through enough."

"It's my job to protect them," Hank said. "And I will."

Some of the energy left Sylvia and she sagged against her husband. "Yes, I know you will. You stood by Amanda. She always told me how you'd be there through thick and thin and..."

Sylvia broke into tears and Ross patted her hand and offered her a tissue.

"Sylvia, I've had to wrestle with it, too. My dating Jolie sort of pushes Amanda out of the way. Like I'm no longer with her. But the truth is, I can't be with her because she's gone. Amanda will always have a part of my heart, but I have more love to give, and she knew that. She didn't want me to drown in the past, but to celebrate life and move forward. That's what's best for me and for my children. That's what I'm going to do."

"Accepting Jolie does seem like a betrayal of sorts," Sylvia admitted.

"I know."

She blew her nose. "You have my blessing," she said finally.

"Thank you," Hank said. "Support us. You'll discover that Jolie's in your corner. Her family is terrific. You'll love them."

"I'll try," Sylvia replied, and with that the conversation moved to other topics before everyone retired for the night.

WHEN THEY REACHED the Tomlinson farm a few minutes after one Saturday afternoon, children were already running everywhere.

"Skip's friends are here, as well," Hank said, and like a bullet, Ethan was gone the minute the car stopped.

Alli lagged behind a bit, ready to play tour guide for her

grandparents. "You should see the foal, Grandmother," she said, tugging Sylvia toward the barn.

"Go ahead," Jolie said. "Alli, after you show your grandparents Starshine, bring them up to the house so they can meet everyone."

"Okay," Alli said, leading her grandparents away.

"YOU SURVIVING so far?" Hank teased two hours later as Jolie finished helping her mother and sister-in-law clean up after they'd all had cake.

"Absolutely." Jolie gave him a quick kiss.

"Hey, we want to play down by the creek," Skip said.

The adults glanced around. "I'll go," Lance offered.

"I can come with you," Jolie said. She leaned over Hank. "I'll help watch them and keep them out of trouble. You can stay here and socialize."

"More like be given the third degree. You should have heard the loaded questions your sister asked when you were in the kitchen."

"I can only imagine. I'll make it up to you later." Jolie ran her fingers across the back of his shoulder.

"You'd better," he teased as she left the room.

She figured he could use the time to talk more with Sylvia and Ross. Hank hadn't filled her in on the details of his conversation with them Friday night, but he'd mentioned it had gone well.

Lance had already left with the boys, so Jolie followed the path down to the creek. Skip and his friends were skipping rocks. A few had waded into the shallow water downstream. No rain had fallen for a week, so the stream meandered; after a storm it could be a raging torrent.

"You and Hank seem to be doing well," Lance said as Jolie stepped onto the gravel bank. The rocks crunched beneath her feet.

"We are," Jolie said. Years of afternoon-recess duty made her locate and place every child. A few boys were swinging on an old tire swing.

"He say those magic words my wife always demands?" Lance asked.

"As a matter of fact, he did," Jolie replied.

Lance whistled. "Never thought I'd see the day. Must have hit his head on something."

Jolie punched him playfully. "Smart-ass."

"And proud of it."

"Hey, Jolie, watch this!" Ethan yelled. He tossed a smooth stone and it skipped about eight times before it lost momentum.

"Nice wrist action," she praised. Ethan hadn't been much of a rock skipper before this summer.

Ethan moved away, perhaps in search of another stone. "So you think you'll marry him?" Lance asked, diverting Jolie's attention.

"I don't know," she said, shrugging. She moved over to help one of the younger boys find a good stone. "You need the flatter and rounder ones," she instructed, moving a bit farther down the gravel bar, her eyes seeking the perfect rock.

"What about this one?" he asked, holding out another.

"No, that won't work." She squatted down.

"Hey, guys, that's not a good idea!" Lance called.

"I found one!" Her charge pressed the stone into Jolie's hand.

Maybe it was teacher's instinct. Maybe it was simply that sixth sense she'd ignored that night long ago when she'd rolled over, assumed all was well and fallen back to sleep. But she knew something was wrong for Lance to have used that tone of voice a second ago.

She straightened and turned toward Lance and the other boys at the same moment she heard him shout another warning.

There was nothing she could do. Five boys had climbed onto the old tire swing. While it could easily have held 250 pounds, the combined weight of the boys clinging to it was well over four hundred. They'd gotten it swinging pretty high, but the height wasn't the issue as the tree branch creaked and moaned under the stress. It was the trajectory. The angle. The way everyone was going to land—on top of Ethan.

She could hear herself scream, felt her feet start to move, but in her heart she knew that no matter how fast she went, she wouldn't be in time.

The crack resounded through the air, the cries of joy turned into panicked yells, and then with a thud, the ground claimed its victims and all was momentarily still.

Chapter Fourteen

A cloud of dust hung over the pile of teenage and preteen boys. Limbs began to untangle as those who'd landed on the others scrambled to their feet and staggered slightly, regaining their footing.

Thank God they hadn't hit the gravel bar. The tire swing went out over a swimming hole on one side and pasture on the other. The boys had hit the area where the grass turned to dirt. No rain meant the ground was packed hard. Still, it was better than landing on sharp rocks.

"Is everyone okay?" Jolie shouted. She and Lance were grabbing the boys, giving them each a cursory once-over as they tried to move them out of the way. The truck tire lay on its side, Ethan trapped underneath.

"Ethan!" Jolie cried.

He didn't respond. His face was pale.

"He's unconscious," Lance stated, lifting the tire. The other boys gathered round. A few were scratched up and one bit back tears as he rubbed his elbow, but it was Ethan who needed help the most.

"Is he going to be okay?" Jolie asked. Adrenaline mixed with fear.

"Of course he is. I just don't know what's wrong with

him yet. He's breathing. Go back to the house and get my truck. Keys are inside. So is my first-aid kit."

Lance was a volunteer firefighter/emergency medical technician for the local fire department.

Jolie paused. "Do we need an ambulance?"

"I can take him faster than Teddy and his crew could get here," Lance told her as she took off at a run and he began his examination.

Jolie hadn't moved this fast in ages and her legs felt as if they were on fire as she raced to where Lance had parked his truck. No one at a Tomlinson farm party worried about car thieves, so the keys were in the ignition. Jolie jumped into the big truck and fired up the engine.

As she put the vehicle in gear, her mother came out onto the porch, wiping her hands on her apron. Jolie didn't have time to explain. Her family would understand something was wrong just by seeing her drive like a bat out of hell toward the creek.

Grass and dirt flew as she tore up the ground of the worn tire tracks leading to where Lance waited. She parked the truck at the edge of the pasture and grabbed Lance's black bag. When she reached Lance, she dropped to her knees beside him. "How is he?"

"I've had him awake once. He hit his head pretty hard. Probably has a concussion, but I don't think he's got any serious brain injury. He also landed on his arm. I felt it, and I think it's broken."

"Not good." Jolie repressed a shudder when she saw that Ethan's arm was bent at an odd angle. She watched as her brother went on checking Ethan. He worked quickly and confidently, and she took comfort in knowing that, as a first responder for a local manufacturing company, Lance received constant medical training.

He managed to get Ethan awake again. "I hurt," Ethan said.

"You hit pretty hard," Lance said. He'd taken off Ethan's shoe and he pinched his toe.

"Ow," Ethan moaned.

Lance gave a sigh of relief. "But you can feel. That's a good sign, Ethan. You hit the ground hard, but you're going to be okay."

"My arm hurts."

"And we're going to go to the hospital and fix that." Lance had gotten Ethan's arm supported and was lifting him. "Let's get him out of here."

The other boys scattered as Lance, with Ethan in his arms, began to stride toward the truck. He reached it at the same time Maudie's Suburban pulled up alongside. Maudie, Bill, Lance's wife, Meg, Hank and his in-laws piled out of the vehicle.

"What's going on?" Maudie said.

Skip stepped forward. "We had too many people on the tire swing and the branch broke."

"Five people," someone chimed in.

"Ethan's hurt," Skip finished.

"What?" This came from Sylvia, who hadn't yet seen her grandson in Lance's arms.

"The tire fell on him." Skip didn't understand he was making the situation worse. "We fell on him. He broke our fall."

"Ethan!" Sylvia shrieked.

Jolie stepped in front of her, blocking her way. "Lance is an EMT. He's taking Ethan to the hospital."

"We need an ambulance." Sylvia's hysteria was increasing.

"Lance has a siren," Maudie said. Her calm voice broke through the din. "He'll get him there. Hank, you and Jolie go with Lance. Bill and I will take the rest of the boys back and make sure they're okay. I can see a few of them have some bruises."

"I'm bleeding." Caught up in the adrenaline rush, Skip hadn't realized he'd hurt himself, and now he stared at his scraped hands.

"You ride with me," Maudie instructed him. "Meg, walk back those who weren't on the tire. The rest, into the Suburban."

As Maudie continued to organize everyone, including Ross and Sylvia, Lance and Hank secured Ethan in the backseat of the cab. Lance slid into the driver's seat. Jolie paused as she approached the truck, unsure of her welcome. But Hank didn't say anything, so she got in the front as he climbed into the back with his son.

Lance threw on the siren and they made it to the hospital in fifteen minutes. As the emergency room wasn't busy, Ethan was quickly through triage. Then the doctor came in, examined him and ordered an X-ray of his arm and back and a CT scan of his head.

Jolie got quietly in a chair in the corner while Lance spoke with the E.R. doctor. Hank gave his insurance card to the registrar, who told him she'd be back to do paperwork later. Ethan had drifted off again, and Hank followed the orderly as he wheeled Ethan out of the E.R. room for more tests.

"I'm going to call Mom," Lance said. Cell phone in his hand, he left the room, too.

Jolie glanced around. The hospital room wasn't large, yet it seemed cavernous now that the bed had been removed. She stood and paced for a few moments.

Hank hadn't spoken to her on the way to the hospital. All his words had been for Ethan. A chill stole over her. She'd failed.

You knew you wouldn't make a good mother.

The voice inside her head that had been biding its time crept back, its tone accusing. Her phone blared Hank's ring tone and despite the signs discouraging cell-phone use, Jolie answered.

"He's getting scanned now," Hank told her. "The doctor thinks it's just a concussion. He's only being cautious."

Hank's attempt at reassurance was as useful as a lead balloon. "This is all my fault," Jolie said.

"Sorry, hold on."

He clicked over and a few minutes later came back onto the line. "Oh, God. Sylvia and Ross just walked through the E.R. entrance. They have Alli with them. This is the last thing I need. God, Jolie, this is a mess. You were supposed to be watching him! Keeping him safe!"

"I'm sorry," Jolie said, his words reverberating in her ears. She hadn't kept Ethan safe. He was injured because of her failure. She'd hurt someone else she loved.

"I have to go," Hank said, disconnecting. She stared at her phone and flipped it closed.

A few minutes later Sylvia, Ross and Alli walked through the door. Jolie wanted to ask why they'd brought Alli, but she already knew the answer. They didn't think she'd be safe on the Tomlinson farm by herself. Alli ran to Jolie and Jolie gathered the little girl in her arms.

"I believe your brother's going to head back to the farm," Sylvia said. "We'll stay here and wait with Hank."

"I want to go back to the farm," Alli said.

"You'll stay with us," Ross told her.

"What about Jolie?" Alli asked, her eyes wide. She was clearly trying to understand the undercurrent traveling among the adults in the room.

"This is a family matter," Sylvia said, her words a knife

to Jolie's heart. "I'm sure Hank will contact you when he knows something."

Jolie turned to Alli and gave her another hug. "You be good for your grandparents. I'll talk to you soon."

Alli's eyes welled up with tears as she realized Jolie was leaving. "Is Ethan going to die? Mommy died in a hospital."

"No, sweetheart. Ethan hit his head and probably broke his arm. He'll have a cast for a few weeks, but he'll be fine."

Alli visibly relaxed. Sylvia came over and put her hand on Alli's shoulder. "Let's go to the cafeteria. We can get something to drink and be back before Ethan gets done in X-ray. Jolie." Sylvia guided her granddaughter out of the room, Ross at their heels.

Jolie's phone rang again. Hank. She stared at it. She'd let him down. She'd let Ethan down. Why had she believed that this time would be different? She was not destined to be a good parent. She was destined to have people hurt on her watch.

She left the room and pressed the button silencing the call.

HANK JABBED the end key on his BlackBerry in frustration. He'd gotten her voice mail. He hadn't meant to be so abrupt, but the radiologist had entered and he'd had to go.

Damn! He replayed the words he'd said over and over in his mind. He'd told her she was supposed to be watching his son. He'd told her she was supposed to be keeping Ethan safe.

How much of an ass could he be? Before he'd dozed off for the nth time, Ethan had woken up long enough to tell Hank a little of what had happened. It'd been a freak accident. So to suggest that Jolie was to blame, his lovely Jolie who had suffered the loss of her child…

He'd realized his mistake the moment the words had left his lips.

Damn, but he was rattled. Maybe it was the way Ethan's arm had dangled. Or how ashen his face had been. Ross and Sylvia's descent on the hospital wasn't helping matters. He could already tell by Sylvia's tone that a lecture was coming.

She'd say this wouldn't have happened if they'd remained in Chicago. He watched as the technician did his thing. Soon they were cleared to go and an orderly wheeled Ethan back to his E.R. room.

"Here you go," the man said, locking the wheels on Ethan's bed. "Your doctor should be in shortly."

"Thanks," Hank replied, too keyed up to sit. He paced the confines, pausing to read labels and signs. But nothing registered except the fact that Jolie wasn't in her chair. At the sound of movement at the door, he turned, but it was only the registrar rolling in her mobile computer. She soon had all the billing information processed and Ethan was officially admitted to the E.R.

A few minutes after the registrar left, Alli and her grandparents walked in. "Hey, Daddy!" Alli rushed up and hugged him. Then she peered over at her brother. "He doesn't look hurt."

"That's because he's asleep," Hank said, trying to keep irritation from seeping into his voice. The hospital was not a place Alli needed to be.

"Ah, it's crowded in here," the doctor said as he walked in. He looked at Alli. "You aren't my patient, are you?" he asked with a wink.

"No." She giggled and pointed at Ethan. "My brother is."

"Ah, should have guessed. You're too perky to be hurt."

Hank knew he was only trying to make the situation lighter. The doctor picked up Ethan's chart. "Mr. Friesen?"

"Yes," Hank said.

The doctor glanced over his shoulder, and Hank coughed. "Sylvia, why don't you and Ross take Alli to the cafeteria?"

"We were just there," Alli said.

"Then the waiting room," Hank said, his gaze not wavering from Amanda's mother. She wasn't happy, but she and Ross left, taking Alli with them.

"Better," the doctor said. "We're going to have to set Ethan's arm. He's broken it, but it's a clean break and nothing that won't heal. No pins necessary and he'll be good as new."

Hank exhaled his relief, and his shoulders sagged as the tension drained away.

"He also has a concussion, but there's nothing on the CT scan to cause us any alarm. He's going to have a nasty headache, but there's no bleeding, swelling or brain trauma."

"Thank God," Hank said. His knees weakened at the good news, and he sank into the chair Jolie had long vacated.

"After we set Ethan's arm we'll watch him for a bit to make sure he doesn't have a bad reaction. The nurse will give you detailed instructions on how to care for both his cast and its removal. We'll also prep you on how to handle his concussion. He's going to have a bad headache. In the old days you had to keep the patient awake, but since we have CT scans now, we can see that there's no brain injury. So you can let him continue to sleep as long as he wants."

Hank nodded. With a cast on his arm, Ethan wouldn't be swimming for a while, but he was going to be okay. It could have been so much worse.

"You'll also want to follow through with your family physician and see if he has any other directives. Most likely he'll want Ethan to come in for a follow-up."

A few weeks ago Hank had gotten the names of some excellent pediatricians from Jolie's siblings, and he'd already made new-patient appointments with one of them. "Okay."

"Great. Let's fix this arm and then we can get you out of here and on your way home. With his exhaustion and the painkillers we've given him, he should hopefully sleep through the procedure."

With that, two nurses appeared and the doctor set about putting the cast on Ethan's forearm. Hank had never broken any bones and the process was fascinating, if a bit horrific, as the doctor applied weights to Ethan's elbow and fingers before setting the arm and forming the cast. As the doctor had predicted, Ethan remained asleep throughout.

Ethan had to stay in the E.R. for a while afterward. The nurses checked on him frequently to make sure he wasn't having any adverse reactions. Then the doctor examined him one last time before discharging him.

Hank and Ethan reached the Nolter and their suite later that night, way past the children's bedtime, and Hank put the still-groggy Ethan to bed. Hank couldn't believe how physically and mentally drained he was. Even Alli had been a bit subdued, albeit curious, as she'd gazed at Ethan's new cast. None of them had eaten a proper meal since lunch, so Hank ordered room service. Ethan needed sleep more than food at the moment, but Hank ordered him some soup in case he woke up hungry.

Hank had lost his appetite, but he forced the food down and tried to keep his anger at Sylvia and Ross in check. Hank's cell phone had been silent—except for a text message from Jolie telling him Ross and Sylvia had told her she should go home. Yet he was even angrier with himself. His last words to Jolie had been those of a man succumbing to an incredibly stressful situation. He knew he'd wounded her and he felt lower than a heel.

"Alli, why don't you go and get ready for bed?" Hank suggested.

His daughter grumbled once but complied. After she left, Hank faced his in-laws. He took a deep breath. "I wish you wouldn't have told Jolie she should go home."

"She's not family," Sylvia said defensively. "You know this wouldn't have happened in Chicago. Hank, you're trying to do too much. You need us. You should consider moving back. Isn't there a position coming open at the home office?"

Hank had no idea if she was simply fishing or if she had inside information. The bottom line was he hadn't made any decisions about his future. Well, not true. He'd made one. But today he'd screwed that up royally. "Look, we're all exhausted. Let's talk tomorrow when we can think straight."

His forehead pounded from a tension headache and he wanted to speak with Jolie. Since Amanda's parents weren't leaving until Monday, he decided to wait until he'd cooled down to discuss things with them. At the moment, with Ethan safe in his own bed, Hank's priority was Jolie. "See you at breakfast," he told them, and strode off to his bedroom. He picked up his bedside phone and dialed.

THE FAMILIAR RING TONE blared through the kitchen of her parents' house and Jolie stopped washing a frying pan and stared at the cell phone resting on the kitchen counter.

"You going to get that?" Maudie asked.

"It's Hank," Jolie said. She'd said little since arriving back at the farm. By now everyone else had cleared out and gone home, but Jolie was unwilling to return to her town house. She didn't want to be alone. Not when she had so much to mull over.

"You need to answer, honey. Find out how Ethan is," Maudie chided gently.

Jolie knew she was right. She wiped her hands on her jeans and grabbed the phone before it trilled its last ring. She pressed the button and answered. "Hi."

"I'm glad I caught you. I've been worried all day," Hank said.

Jolie held the phone to her ear as she left the kitchen, seeking the privacy of her childhood bedroom. "How's Ethan?"

"He's going to be fine. He has a broken arm, but it was a clean break. Nothing major. Six weeks in a cast and all should be well. He has a concussion but no swelling, bleeding or anything like that. Really, aside from feeling as if a tire and five boys fell on him, he's going to be good as new."

"I'm sorry," she blurted as tears came. "I only turned my back for a few minutes. I didn't realize they'd all climbed on. It was stupid. My fault. I should have—"

"It was an accident," Hank said. "I had no right to say what I did to you. I was so afraid and overwhelmed that I lashed out. I'm so sorry."

"You had every right. Ethan got hurt because of me. Had the swing landed on him when he was on the gravel bar, he could have died. He could have *died.* Because of me." Her voice cracked and despair consumed her. She'd been pretending she was something she wasn't. She wasn't destined to be happy. Hadn't she made her peace with that? Accepted she'd pay penance for her baby's death for the rest of her days?

"Jolie," Hank said, but his voice seemed distant as the dark cloud she'd been trying to escape from under claimed her. Ethan, whom she loved, had been hurt on her watch. She would never forgive herself.

"Jolie." Hank called her name again, but Jolie knew it was too late.

“I can’t do this anymore,” she told him.

“What do you mean?”

“This. Us.” Her voice came out ragged as if she’d run out of breath. “I can’t deal with people I love getting hurt. I’m bad luck. You deserve better.”

“You’re being irrational. I love you. These things happen. They’re normal. How many broken bones did your brothers have?”

Hank made sense, but Sylvia’s censure and Hank’s thoughtless words had opened deep psychological wounds. She’d already been through all the stages of grief. The guilt. The despair. The pain and finally the letting go. Today had been a wake-up call. She couldn’t ever set herself up for that kind of pain again.

“Hank, I’m sorry. I can’t. Not now. I…I have to go.” Jolie pressed the button on the phone before her nerve failed her. He called her back twice, left her two messages. But she ignored them.

Today had shown her she’d been deluding herself. Time to get over the fantasy and move on.

Chapter Fifteen

Sunday dawned, one of those perfect summer days. Temperatures reached the low nineties and a light breeze made being outside a joy. As Hank returned from a late-morning run, he wiped the sweat from his brow and reflected on the past twelve hours. He'd been up all night thinking. And when he'd finally gone to bed he'd slept maybe an hour or two without tossing and turning. He'd risen early, made a phone call and gotten Peter out of bed. His boss hadn't been happy, but twenty years of friendship granted Hank a few liberties, and Peter understood once Hank told him what had happened.

By the end of the hour-long phone call Hank had made his decision. They were moving. He'd shared the information with Ross and Sylvia and the twins over breakfast. Ethan hadn't felt like eating much, but he was up, aware and recovering. Alli had been her normal, chipper self, not upset with the decision at all. She'd reminded Hank she had a piano lesson, which was her main concern.

After yesterday's events, Hank wasn't sure how welcome any visit to the farm would be, so he'd called Maudie. The lesson was still on for two o'clock.

Hank showered and changed, feeling revived from his run. He wanted to talk to Jolie. She had a right to know what he'd decided, especially now that he'd told his children. He tried her cell phone but she didn't answer.

Alli and Hank left for the farm around one-thirty. Ethan was improving as the day wore on, and Ross and Sylvia were keeping him company.

Hank pulled up the drive, parked and ushered Alli into the house. He'd noticed Jolie's car outside. "Is she here?" he asked Maudie.

Maudie opened a piano book and settled Alli down in front of the instrument before replying. She led Hank to a window. "See that path? The one between those two tall rosebushes?"

He'd noticed the path leading into a garden before, but hadn't really paid much attention or checked it out. "I see it."

"Follow it to the end. You'll find her." Maudie moved to a chair near Alli. "Very good. I can tell you've been practicing."

Hank left the farmhouse by a side door. He'd never been here when the place was still. Animals moved about and butterflies fluttered, but no children raced around. The effect was a bit unsettling.

He crossed the short expanse of lawn and found the stepping stones that led into the garden. In Chicago his house had had a few flower beds, but this rivaled something you'd see at a botanical garden.

After walking a few feet he realized why.

He'd stepped into the Tomlinson family plot. He passed the headstone of someone named Myra, who died in 1934. Then he paused and looked around, seeing small markers popping out between well-laid flower beds and grassy areas. He knew why Jolie was here and it broke his heart.

He traveled deeper into the garden, the markers getting newer. The farm was more than a hundred years old. Its first occupants had arrived in the early 1900s. He should have known her child would be here and not in some public graveyard.

His footsteps alerted her to his presence, and she turned from where she'd been weeding. She'd torn the creeping vines away from the tiny headstone. "What are you doing here?" she demanded.

"Alli had a piano lesson. Your mom told me where you were."

"Oh." She seemed angry. Defensive. She'd built up the walls around her heart. They were walls he knew she really didn't want. Walls that yesterday he'd helped to rebuild. Walls that today he planned to tear down.

"We have to talk," he stated.

"There's nothing to say." She wiped her forehead with the back of her hand, spreading dirt particles on her skin.

"Actually, there is." He stepped forward. "I'm not going to let you do this."

She stared at him. "There's nothing you can do. My mind is made up."

"No," Hank said. He was ready to argue. Ready to fight. "You've grieved long enough." He read the name on the gravestone. Ruthie Marie. "I bet she was pretty."

"The most beautiful baby ever. She was the best thing I'd ever done." Her lower lip quivered and he longed to touch her, make her demons vanish.

"I always thought marrying Amanda was the best thing I'd ever done. Turns out life doesn't limit you to doing just one best thing."

"Maybe your life," she replied, not giving an inch.

"You don't think my world fell apart?" Hank demanded. "I had time to say goodbye, but nothing I did could prepare me for what came next. It took five years before I could think about stepping out on my own."

"Everyone thought I should get over it and move on," Jolie said.

"I told them to go to hell," Hank said fiercely.

"I didn't have the guts," Jolie admitted.

"No, you buried it within yourself. You blamed yourself. You still do. And that's why I'm here. Because I'm not going to let your fear destroy our relationship."

"What?" Her mouth gaped. He'd shocked her. Good.

"I love you. You're afraid of what the future might bring. That if you let someone close to you you're going to get hurt. The pain will be unbearable. It's better to end a relationship than to face the problems head-on. Better to hurt in a small way than to risk the pain of losing someone you love."

She sputtered and he refused to let her get a word in edgewise. "Someone told me at Amanda's funeral that God doesn't take someone unless his or her time is done. It didn't make sense to me then. I don't remember who said it, but I know she was trying to offer comfort. She meant that Amanda's job on this earth was done."

"That's morbid."

He nodded. "In a sense. It's a new way of thinking. People always say, 'How terrible. They had so much left to give.' But maybe not. Maybe all they were here to do is done. Maybe Amanda's purpose in this world was to give birth to two incredible kids and show me a taste of happiness. I'm not even going to speculate on Ruthie. But I know her purpose wasn't to make you afraid to love again."

"And that's it?"

Hank shrugged. "How would I have known that I'd found happiness again if I hadn't found it once with Amanda?"

"I thought my life would be so different," Jolie said, tears streaming down her cheeks.

"And long ago I believed the same. So let's make a pledge. From this point forward, I'm not going to give up on our future because you're afraid. I'm going to fight you all the way because I love you and you belong at my side just as I belong at yours. I'm telling you, Jolie, the rest of our lives is going to burst with the good stuff. And for those few rare times we hit a bump in the road, or a broken arm, or a concussion, we'll stand together through it."

"Whoa." She staggered a bit and then sank to her knees next to the grave.

Hank came closer and hunkered down next to her. "You okay?"

"Overwhelmed." She wiped her eyes with the back of her hands, trying to banish her tears without leaving streaks of dirt. "I thought you'd hate me. I let you down. You snapped at me."

"A momentary aberration brought on by Ross and Sylvia's unwelcome presence. It was you I wanted and needed. If you hadn't been there to help Lance, everything could have been worse. The doctor said your and Lance's quick actions helped immensely."

"Oh. But Sylvia—"

"I know what Sylvia did. She projected her own fears. She wants me to move back to Chicago. Well, we're moving all right, but—"

"What? You can't!"

Hank chuckled. "And you were telling me to go?" She smacked him on the arm.

"I do love you," she said. "So much. I was out of my mind yesterday. Losing Ruthie... Then the thought of losing Ethan. I couldn't handle it."

"Love is risk, but it's the best kind and I'm willing to risk with you. I am moving, but so are you. And not to Chicago, but in with me, into a house, here in Branson."

"But living together, that's..."

He loved her sense of propriety. "I love you. I want you in my life—as my wife. We're getting married. If you'll have me."

"We are?" She sniffled. Hank settled down beside her and cradled her in his arms.

"Jolie, I want to spend the rest of my life with you. We can work out the details later. But in my heart, you've become my other half. You're the one I want to see when I wake up and the one I want to kiss before I go to sleep. You make me feel alive."

"The other shoe always drops," she tried.

"And it will, but we'll pick it up together," Hank said. "You aren't leaving me."

"No," she said.

"And you know where this is going to lead, to that happily-ever-after part like in Alli's books."

"Uh-huh," she said.

"Then will you kiss me now? Because I really need to touch you. I really need you to reassure me that we're going to be okay."

"We are," she told him, and she brought her lips to his.

AS SHE KISSED Hank, a contentment Jolie hadn't experienced before stole over her. He'd seen her at her worst. He'd seen her panic. Seen her fears. He hadn't run. Instead, he'd fought for her. And he'd owned his own mistakes. He was a good man and a good partner.

The future would always be uncertain. But Hank's love was something she could bank on. She could feel it in the way he held her close, the way he tenderly wiped the dirt smudges from her face.

Maybe you had to endure some heartache to really appreciate the good times. Maybe life didn't always turn out the way you'd planned or anticipated.

She might be a teacher, but today Hank had taught her the greatest lesson of all. Sometimes love came when you least expected it.

Epilogue

Almost six years later

"Are you ready?" Ethan pounded on Alli's bedroom door. You'd think she'd realize how important this day was. It wasn't every day they turned sixteen or their little brother and sister turned three. Ethan still wasn't sure how it had happened: that his dad and Jolie had had twins on his and Alli's birthday in September. Four people having the same birthday in one family just seemed a little strange.

Heck, Jolie had even delivered the babies naturally; they hadn't been scheduled to arrive for another few weeks.

Ethan had learned all about the reproductive system in health class. Most of his friends found his enthusiasm for the subject a bit weird. Guys his age liked the idea of sex, but weren't really interested in the anatomically correct, book part. That made Ethan an oddity. Perhaps he'd changed, because since the bump on the head and the broken arm, he'd wanted to become a doctor. Now a junior in high school, he took every science class he could.

"Come on, Alli! We're going to be late for the party at the farm. I heard we might get a car."

That got her out the door fast. "A car?"

"A junk heap, probably, like everyone else in this family got for their first car, but a car nonetheless. I've got to earn money for college and I'm tired of borrowing Dad's car to get to work. You could use some money, too. If we only get one car, we'll have to share."

"I'm doing child care at the Nolter after school. You know I'm thinking about being a teacher. Dad can take me to work. But don't think you'll get the car all the time."

She adjusted a strand of her hair and Ethan grimaced. His sister had started primping constantly. Worse, his best friends thought she was hot. He had no idea what they saw in her.

They tromped downstairs, where Jolie was trying to corral two racing toddlers. Bryce had taken Emily's toy and she was chasing him. Hank arrived and scooped up his youngest daughter, diverting her from the tackle she was about to make on her brother.

"Are we ready? Everyone's probably out at the farm by now," Jolie said.

"It's not like we have that far to go," Hank reminded her.

"I guess not." Jolie glanced at her shirt, which now had a stain on it. "You go on ahead. I'll walk through the pasture in a few minutes after I change."

Alli took Bryce, and Hank toted out a laughing Emily. "You going to be okay?" Ethan called. He really did love Jolie. He and Alli had discussed it when the twins had arrived. They'd really been blessed.

"I'll be right behind you," Jolie told him.

She watched as Ethan went outside before she turned and ran upstairs. She did only have a few hundred yards to go, although it was through a grove of trees and a horse pasture.

Like Bill's, her and Hank's acreage bordered the Tomlinson farm. When they'd decided to look for a house, the farm next door to her parents' had come up for sale. Fate, Jolie had realized. She'd married Hank six months after Ethan broke his arm and never looked back. Even Sylvia and Ross had accepted her, and considered themselves grandparents of four, not just two. They were already at the farm, having driven out from their suite at the Nolter where they'd moved four years ago. They'd settled into retired life with gusto, and were probably more active than Hank and Jolie, whose ideal night involved snuggling up with a movie and popcorn.

She changed her shirt and glanced out the bedroom window. She should have heard gravel crunching by now, but Hank hadn't even gotten the car started. He was still trying to strap two wriggling and excited toddlers into their car seats. Ethan and Alli were already in the third row of the hybrid Tahoe. Hank looked up, saw her watching and smiled. She knew he'd wait until she climbed in before he'd leave.

She shook her head at her good fortune. He loved her so very much. He'd even gotten up every night that first year to check on their children. He'd understood her fear. He'd helped her conquer it. He was her other half.

A grin spread across her face as she raced down the stairs to the man who'd made all her dreams come true.

* * * * *

Celebrate 60 years of pure reading pleasure
with Harlequin®!
Silhouette® Romantic Suspense is celebrating
with the glamour-filled, adrenaline-charged series
LOVE IN 60 SECONDS
starting in April 2009.
Six stories that promise to bring the glitz of Las Vegas,
the danger of revenge, the mystery of a missing diamond,
family scandals and ripped-from-the-headlines intrigue.
Get your heart racing as love happens in sixty seconds!

Enjoy a sneak peek of
USA TODAY *bestselling author Marie Ferrarella's*
THE HEIRESS'S 2-WEEK AFFAIR.
Available April 2009
from Silhouette® Romantic Suspense.

Eight years ago Matt Shaffer had vanished out of Natalie Rothchild's life, leaving behind a one-line note tucked under a pillow that had grown cold: *I'm sorry, but this just isn't going to work.*

That was it. No explanation, no real indication of remorse. The note had been as clinical and compassionless as an eviction notice, which, in effect, it had been, Natalie thought as she navigated through the morning traffic. Matt had written the note to evict her from his life.

She'd spent the next two weeks crying, breaking down without warning as she walked down the street, or as she sat staring at a meal she couldn't bring herself to eat.

Candace, she remembered with a bittersweet pang, had tried to get her to go clubbing in order to get her to forget about Matt.

She'd turned her twin down, but she did get her act together. If Matt didn't think enough of their relationship to try to contact her, to try to make her understand why he'd changed so radically from lover to stranger, then to hell with him. He was dead to her, she resolved. And he'd remained that way.

Until twenty minutes ago.

The adrenaline in her veins kept mounting.

Natalie focused on her driving. Vegas in the daylight wasn't nearly as alluring, as magical and glitzy as it was after dark. Like an aging woman best seen in soft lighting, Vegas's imperfections were all visible in the daylight. Natalie supposed that was why people like her sister didn't like to get up until noon. They lived for the night.

Except that Candace could no longer do that.

The thought brought a fresh, sharp ache with it.

"Damn it, Candy, what a waste," Natalie murmured under her breath.

She pulled up before the Janus casino. One of the three valets currently on duty came to life and made a beeline for her vehicle.

"Welcome to the Janus," the young attendant said cheerfully as he opened her door with a flourish.

"We'll see," she replied solemnly.

As he pulled away with her car, Natalie looked up at the casino's logo. Janus was the Roman god with two faces, one pointed toward the past, the other facing the future. It struck her as rather ironic, given what she was doing here, seeking out someone from her past in order to get answers so that the future could be settled.

The moment she entered the casino, the Vegas phenomena took hold. It was like stepping into a world where time did not matter or even make an appearance. There was only a sense of "now."

Because in Natalie's experience she'd discovered that bartenders knew the inner workings of any establishment they worked far better than anyone else, she made her way to the first bar she saw within the casino.

The bartender in attendance was a gregarious man in his early forties. He had a quick, sexy smile, which was probably one of the main reasons he'd been hired. His name tag identified him as Kevin.

Moving to her end of the bar, Kevin asked, "What'll it be, pretty lady?"

"Information." She saw a dubious look cross his brow. To counter that, she took out her badge. Granted she wasn't here in an official capacity, but Kevin didn't need to know that. "Were you on duty last night?"

Kevin began to wipe the gleaming black surface of the bar. "You mean during the gala?"

"Yes."

The smile gracing his lips was a satisfied one. Last night had obviously been profitable for him, she judged. "I caught an extra shift."

She took out Candace's photograph and carefully placed it on the bar. "Did you happen to see this woman there?"

The bartender glanced at the picture. Mild interest turned to recognition. "You mean Candace Rothchild? Yeah, she was here, loud and brassy as always. But not for long," he added, looking rather disappointed. There was always a circus when Candace was around, Natalie thought. "She and the boss had at it and then he had our head of security escort her out."

She latched on to the first part of his statement. "They argued? About what?"

He shook his head. "Couldn't tell you. Too far away for anything but body language," he confessed.

"And the head of security?" she asked.

"He got her to leave."

She leaned in over the bar. "Tell me about him."

"Don't know much," the bartender admitted. "Just that his name's Matt Shaffer. Boss flew him in from L.A., where he was head of security for Montgomery Enterprises."

There was no avoiding it, she thought darkly. She was going to have to talk to Matt. The thought left her cold. "Do you know where I can find him right now?"

Kevin glanced at his watch. "He should be in his office. On the second floor, toward the rear." He gave her the numbers of the rooms where the monitors that kept watch over the casino guests as they tried their luck against the house were located.

Taking out a twenty, she placed it on the bar. "Thanks for your help."

Kevin slipped the bill into his vest pocket. "Anytime, lovely lady," he called after her. "Anytime."

She debated going up the stairs, then decided on the elevator. The car that took her up to the second floor was empty. Natalie stepped out of the elevator, looked around to get her bearings and then walked toward the rear of the floor.

"Into the Valley of Death rode the six hundred," she silently recited, digging deep for a line from a poem by Tennyson. Wrapping her hand around a brass handle, she opened one of the glass doors and walked in.

The woman whose desk was closest to the door looked up. "You can't come in here. This is a restricted area."

Natalie already had her ID in her hand and held it up. "I'm looking for Matt Shaffer," she told the woman.

God, even saying his name made her mouth go dry. She was supposed to be over him, to have moved on with her life. What happened?

The woman began to answer her. "He's—"

"Right here."

The deep voice came from behind her. Natalie felt every single nerve ending go on tactical alert at the same moment that all the hairs at the back of her neck stood up. Eight years had passed, but she would have recognized his voice anywhere.

* * * * *

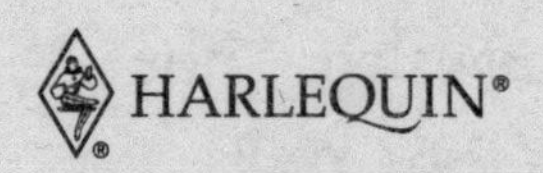

COMING NEXT MONTH

Available April 14, 2009

#1253 A COWBOY'S PROMISE by Marin Thomas
Men Made in America
Keeping her Idaho horse farm going has been a struggle for Amy Olsen. Then ex-rodeo rider Matt Cartwright shows up to collect on a debt. But once he meets the widow and her two young daughters, Matt's the one who wants to make good. And when he finds himself falling for Amy, making good is one promise he intends to keep!

#1254 FOUND: ONE BABY by Cathy Gillen Thacker
Made in Texas
From the moment she comes to the rescue of an abandoned infant on her neighbor's porch, Michelle Anderson is smitten. But when the sexy doctor next door, Thad Garner, proposes they join together to adopt the baby, Michelle refuses to marry without love. So Thad must prove to her that "love, marriage, baby" can work out—even if you do it in the wrong order!

#1255 MISTLETOE CINDERELLA by Tanya Michaels
4 Seasons in Mistletoe
When Dylan Echols mistakes her for the most popular girl in high school at their ten-year reunion, Chloe Malcolm seizes the Cinderella moment. The small-town computer programmer has had a crush on the former big-league pitcher since forever. But what happens once the clock strikes twelve? Will she turn back into her tongue-tied former self? Or have a happily-ever-after with the prince of her dreams?

#1256 THE GOOD FATHER by Kara Lennox
Second Sons
The last thing Max Remington wants is to get involved with Jane Selwyn. Not only does she work for him, but she's a single mom! It's not that he doesn't like kids, but they complicate things. And his top priority is building his advertising agency. Too bad his heart won't listen to his head....